CW00506437

A gripping mystery inspired by the work of Sir Arthur Conan Doyle

THE ILLUMINATION OF SHERLOCK HOLMES

The Odyssey of Sherlock Holmes Trilogy: Book 3

PAUL D. GILBERT

JOFFE
BOOKS

First published in Great Britain 2019
Joffe Books, London

This book is a work of fiction. Names, characters, businesses,
organisations, places and events are either the product of the
author's imagination or are used fictitiously. Any resemblance
to actual persons, living or dead, events or locales is entirely
coincidental. The spelling used is British English except where
fidelity to the author's rendering of accent or dialect
supersedes this. The right of Paul D. Gilbert to be identified
as author of this work has been asserted by him in accordance
with the Copyright, Designs and Patents Act 1988.

© Paul D. Gilbert

**Please join our mailing list for free Kindle crime thriller,
detective, and mystery books and new releases.**

www.joffebooks.com

ISBN 978-1-78931-190-7

Only time and, of course, my readers, will be the judge of whether the concept of a trilogy was a well conceived one or not. Nevertheless, I trust that each instalment, including this the third and final one, can stand on its own merit as an individual novel, which had always been my original intention.

It's been a long journey and I sincerely hope that you all find the completed work as satisfying to read as I have found it to write, and I beg from you a little sympathy for my long-suffering wife and mentor, Jackie.

Paul D. Gilbert

FOREWORD

The events of the last few months have been so dramatic and occurred with such a momentum that, at times, they feel like a dream whenever I try to assimilate them.

As always, it has been a privilege to observe my friend, Mr Sherlock Holmes, exercise the incredible powers with which he has been endowed, and the rapid succession of cases that have been brought to the door of our lodgings at 221B Baker Street, have extended them to their very limits.

Our journeys to Rome and Egypt, in pursuit of a ruthless murderer and an ancient manuscript, the contents of which threatened to shake our accepted institutions to their very foundations, saw us return to London in a state of physical and mental exhaustion.

However, my friend's limitless enthusiasm and energy allowed him to throw himself at each new problem as if it had been his first. As this series of events progressed, he began to sense that every one of these cases, despite their nature being so apparently disparate, were somehow connected and that they were leading him upon a single path that was not of his choosing.

Holmes had persuaded Inspectors Lestrade and Bradstreet of Scotland Yard to abandon their cherished protocols and to throw in their lot with us. Before long, they began to share his conviction that the inestimable organisation that had been behind the events in both Rome and Egypt had also been manipulating these events in London.

The myriad of connections, between the players of this dangerous game and the Diogenes Club, were now causing Mycroft Holmes the gravest concern. After all, Mycroft had been one of the London club's founding members and his cherished anonymity had now been thrown into jeopardy.

Even he, despite the vast network of agents that served him as a senior member of the British Government and the information that was placed on his desk in Whitehall on a daily basis, had not deduced the size and influence of this malevolent Brotherhood.

Each of Holmes's fresh discoveries had led him to one inevitable conclusion. However, his brother had already arrived at his, and Mycroft's subsequent disappearance had shaken Holmes to the core. To my dismay, Holmes had immediately decided to follow suit and without a moment's notice. Consequently, I knew that I had much work to do if I were to pick up their trail in time . . .

John H. Watson

CHAPTER ONE

THE DARK ENTITY

The night before my departure had proved to be a long and restless one, and the little sleep that I did finally fall into had been fitful and clouded by anxiety.

Eventually I gave up the ghost and abandoned my bed for the armchair in our sitting room. As I sat there with a pipe, the cause of my fretfulness suddenly emerged from my subconscious and I leapt over to my desk. I rummaged through my manuscripts in a desperate effort at confirming this sudden realisation of mine and I soon emerged triumphant, clutching the sought after papers in my fist.

Initially, I could not be sure as to why the affair of Wilson, the notorious canary trainer, should seem so relevant to the quest that now lay ahead of me. Therefore, I decided to read it through in its entirety, or at least until its pertinence became more obvious to me.

> As I look back through my notes for the autumn of 1895, I realise that the glut of cases, with which my good friend Sherlock Holmes and I had been inundated, will provide me with enough source

material for my humble literary offerings for some time to come.

A brief respite had allowed Holmes the opportunity to resume his violin compositions, but that was a process that did not exactly induce an atmosphere in which I could proceed with my own form of creativity. I tried my best to block out the discordant screeching that Holmes's beleaguered instrument had been continuously forced to produce. However, I soon realised that my references to the strange affairs I have chronicled under the headings of 'The Nervous Mariner' and 'The Armour of Charlemagne' would remain as nothing more than that, unless my friend postponed his torturous recitals!

'Really Holmes, I am certain that even Beethoven must have given himself and those around him an occasional hiatus from his great works!' I protested while slamming my notebook shut with violent frustration. I was relieved and surprised to note that Holmes was prepared to respond to my outburst in an unexpectedly affable manner.

'Oh, my dear fellow, I did not realise that my harmless attempts at musical composition would provide you with such distress. Naturally, I shall cease at once.' Holmes smiled and placed his violin back upon its rest.

'Holmes, I do apologise, but you must realise that you were making it nigh on impossible for me to concentrate upon my notes.'

Holmes dismissed my attempt at appeasement with a dramatic flourish of his arm as he moved over to the fireplace. From the mantelpiece he collected together all the plugs and dottels from his smokes of the previous evening and then put a light to this, his first pipe of the day.

I am ashamed to admit that it was almost noon before our breakfast table was finally cleared that day and Holmes was still clad in his favourite purple dressing gown. Although it is true to say that, when not gainfully employed, Holmes and I tended to keep the most Bohemian of hours, on this occasion, I fear that we had overstepped the mark somewhat.

Then I noticed that Holmes was employing his rosewood pipe and I knew at once that I could expect a rather disputatious conversation from my friend. In this, I was not to be disappointed.

'So, Doctor, which of our recent adventures do you intend to embellish and romanticise, before inflicting the results upon your long-suffering readers?' I could tell from his tone that Holmes was determined to take out his creative frustrations upon my own humble efforts. Nevertheless, I was not going to sit idly by while he censured my writing skills once again.

'Really Holmes,' I began, 'I do not consider my attempts at making your demonstrations a little less dry and more readable as mere embellishments! Surely you cannot raise any objections to having our adventures and your skills as a detective reach a wider readership?'

'What difference does it make so long as this larger audience of yours fails to appreciate the subtleties and nuances of the science of deduction? Your intention should be to broaden the understanding of observation and reason, rather than to diminish it. I mean to say, just look at this!' Holmes threw down my recently completed manuscript for *The Giant Rat of Sumatra* upon the dining table.

'You have me here, for example, slithering around upon the deck of the *Matilda Briggs* like some predatory reptile, whereas in actual fact I was engaged in the most intricate exercise of observation and deduction. You describe the weather in the most

9

engaging and dramatic fashion while, all the while, I was below deck delving into the unlocked secrets contained within the bowels of that most mysterious and tragic ship. Thrill your readers if you must, but do not denigrate my art and science by passing them off as some form of cheap theatrical display!'

I had been so completely taken aback by this outburst, Holmes's most vitriolic attack to date, that I could not, in all honesty, offer a single word of response in my own defence.

'Well, I am certain that my sorely put-upon public will appreciate your most considered and valued critique!' I am ashamed to admit that this feeble and sarcastic response was all that I was able to muster.

Mercifully, this acerbic encounter of ours was brought to a premature but welcome conclusion by our landlady Mrs Hudson announcing the arrival of our former antagonist, Inspector Lestrade of Scotland Yard.

I say 'former antagonist', because by this stage in our association both Holmes and the nervous inspector had garnered a form of mutual respect from the other. Ever since the investigation into the most singular events of The Affair of the Six Busts of Napoleon, Holmes had come to realise, from Lestrade's heartfelt admission, that Scotland Yard no longer felt any resentment at his interventions; rather, it had evolved into the utmost respect and appreciation.

On this occasion, Lestrade's hangdog features were further contorted by an anxiety that I had not previously witnessed upon them. Recognising this at once, Holmes immediately showed the troubled inspector over to a chair by the fire with a dramatic flourish of his right arm and then, despite the hour, he poured him out a generous measure from our port decanter and offered him a cigar. Lestrade readily accepted them both.

Holmes allowed the inspector time enough to relish both offerings before broaching the subject of his reason for this unexpected visit.

'So, Inspector Lestrade, I perceive that we are not being honoured by a social visit on this occasion.' Holmes pointed towards the policeman's notebook, which was protruding rather precariously from the top of his coat pocket.

Lestrade was visibly embarrassed by Holmes's declaration and he did not hesitate for a moment in confirming the accuracy of the observation. He nodded emphatically while putting a light to his cigar.

'I would have been glad had it been a social visit, Mr Holmes, but sadly nothing could be further from the truth.'

After a sip or two from his port, Lestrade became more conducive to the idea of voicing his concerns.

'What do you know of the individual who goes by the name of Wilson the canary trainer?' he asked bluntly.

Holmes jerked his head in the direction of the bookshelf beside the fireplace that contained our indexes. I pulled down the file marked 'W' and began to turn over those well-thumbed pages. I slapped my hand upon the relevant page to confirm my success.

'I have it!' I announced. 'It states simply: "Wilson, the notorious canary trainer, who is also known as the Black Plague of East London."'[1]

---

[1] From 'Sherlock Holmes and the Adventure of the Black Plague' by P.D.G. and 'The Adventure of Black Peter' by Sir A.C.D.

'Oh, so you already know him as such?' Lestrade asked, clearly surprised by the data that was at our disposal.

'It is our business to have as clear an understanding of the criminal world as is possible,' I said proudly, returning the index to its shelf.

'I also seem to recollect,' Holmes stated sharply, turning towards the troubled policeman, 'that you placed him under arrest a full year ago, Inspector! I fail to see why you have come to us upon the matter at this late stage.'

Lestrade was clearly uncomfortable with this revelation and he shifted in his chair several times before replying.

'That is true, Mr Holmes, but unfortunately the evidence against him was insufficient for a conviction. The man is the vilest exponent of extortion and he utilizes every sort of threat and violence in order to obtain his ill-gotten gains. Obviously, his canary emporium is but a facade for his real trade. He employs the worst kind of hoodlum to visit every tradesman in the area on the last day of every month. He sets a price based on the type of business concerned, but if the payment is not immediately forthcoming, his men are instructed to cause as much damage to the premises as is possible. Unfortunately, if his men continue to return empty-handed then it is the proprietor himself who feels his wrath!

'The rogue makes no secret of his malicious profession, so a warrant for his arrest is never hard to obtain. However, by the time that the case finally comes to court, each witness receives another visit and is left in no doubt as to the dire consequences of his giving evidence against Wilson or his men. Subsequently, each case against him breaks down as soon as a witness is called. No one dare say a word against him and my superiors are unrelenting in their demands for a conviction, I don't mind telling you.

'So I have come to you, Mr Holmes,' finished Lestrade, flushed and breathless, 'as I have on so many previous occasions, in the hope that you might find a solution to my dilemma.'

Holmes smiled sympathetically and immediately swapped his rosewood pipe for his old clay. He drew on this long and hard before responding to Lestrade's request.

'I have the utmost sympathy for you, Inspector Lestrade,' he began, 'but I fail to see what it is that you expect me to do. Clearly there is no new evidence that I can accrue on your behalf and I certainly cannot force your witnesses to give evidence against their will. Yet such a creature as this Wilson cannot and must not be allowed to continue.'

'The scoundrel!' I blurted out my indignation with understandable ferocity, but Holmes hushed me with a movement of his hand. He moved lazily over to the window and smoked in silence, clearly lost in concentration.

'There is nothing else for it . . .' He said this more to himself than to either of us and his voice was barely audible.

Suddenly he returned to the centre of the room and his eyes flared with excitement. He pulled Lestrade back up on to his feet and began to usher him towards the door.

'Inspector, you shall hear from me within forty-eight hours, but I warn you that a long and dangerous night's work lies ahead of you!'

The inspector appealed to me for an explanation as he opened the door to leave, but I merely shrugged my shoulders, for I had none. Upon Lestrade's departure, Holmes wasted no time in dashing off to his room, the door slamming resoundingly behind him.

For a few minutes a perplexing cacophony of sounds reverberated from behind the door as Holmes conducted a hurried and haphazard search through his drawers and cupboards. When he did eventually emerge, his transformation was as startling as it was complete.

Indeed, Holmes's mutation had been so thorough that his laugh upon seeing my look of amazement was that of a bucolic and elderly tinker! He had taken a full six inches off of his height and somehow his self-imposed stoop conjured up the humped back of a man used to bending over for hours on end while he went about his craft.

Holmes's hair now protruded below the rim of his crumpled, old brown hat and it was a dirty silver grey in colour. His elongated nose sported a lacerated and congealing boil and his lips were cracked and red. He sported a battered old greatcoat and a stained overall. The final touch was a pair of steel rimmed spectacles, that were perched precariously on the edge of his nose. When he smiled, however, he was unmistakable to me, even through this disguise.

'So, Watson, do you find my new persona satisfactory?' he asked superfluously.

'It is wondrous, Holmes, as well you know, and I would not have recognised you had I not been witness to this miracle. For the life of me, however, I cannot imagine why you have gone to such lengths,' I ventured, although without any real hope of receiving an explanation from my friend.

'Very likely not,' said he, 'but suffice it to say that you would certainly not approve were you to be privy to my intention. I cannot venture a time for my return, but I would strongly advise you to take all necessary precautions during my absence.' By this I knew him to mean that I should clean and load my old army revolver, in preparation for an imminent, but as yet, unidentifiable new adventure.

Then, without another word or a moment's further delay, Holmes was gone and I went upstairs to fetch my weapon from its drawer.

* * *

The next twenty-four hours passed very slowly indeed and I lost count of the number of times that I cleaned my revolver during that long wait. My meals, and Mrs Hudson, came and went with regularity and the papers were without any real points of interest. The cold, damp weather precluded any thoughts of a long walk and I had not the patience for a book. Twenty-four hours became forty-eight and finally, when I was beginning to despair of ever seeing my friend again, my lonely reverie was broken by a terrible commotion at the street door.

I raced down the stairs and was immediately met by a sight that shook me to the core! Sherlock Holmes was leaning upon Mrs Hudson's shoulder for support and, even with her assistance, I struggled to heave his listless form up the stairs to our rooms.

Holmes attempted an ironic smile at the sight of my concern and despite the visual evidence to the contrary, he insisted that his appearance should be of no cause for concern. Obviously, I begged to differ and after gently ushering a despairing Mrs Hudson out of the room, I immediately set to work at removing the vestiges of his bedraggled disguise while causing as little further damage as possible.

His wounds were many, but thankfully mostly superficial. His coat was stained with blood down one side, where he had obviously taken a kick or two from a steel capped boot. There was severe bruising around and above both eyes and his lips were a bloody mess.

Clearly he was in no condition to answer any of my myriad of questions so I worked upon him in silence with my bottle of iodine, some lint and bandages obtained from my medical bag. Finally, I completed my treatment with a generous helping of brandy, which I fed to him slowly where he lay upon the chaise longue.

As a precaution, I decided to leave him there overnight, rather than force him to struggle into his room. To my surprise, he was still there the following morning and his wounds were already on the mend. Holmes sat up to greet me, clearly aware of the progress that he had made.

'Watson, you are indeed a most excellent medical practitioner, I must say.'

'Thank you, Holmes; although your remarkable recuperative powers deserve as much credit as my own skills.'

'You do not do your abilities full justice, Watson, and on further consideration I must confess that my assessment of your writing abilities may also have been somewhat wide of the mark,' he admitted sheepishly. Then he paused for a moment.

'My dear Watson, although your concern for my welfare is undoubtedly most admirable, one should not lose sight of the fact that the process of actually caring is detrimental to the pursuit of pure logical progression.'

Naturally I was on the point of raising my objections to Holmes's flagrant dismissal of the virtues of human compassion, when to my surprise he suddenly expressed an unusual eagerness for his breakfast. When it did finally appear, he devoured his ham and eggs voraciously.

'Nothing quite builds up an appetite like a sound thrashing!' He laughed in acknowledgement of my look of surprise.

'Well, I must confess that I would rather not eat for a week than endure what you have been through,' I responded. Holmes dismissed this with a smile.

It was only once the breakfast things had been removed and we were both lighting our cigarettes that Holmes decided to divulge the chain of events that had led to his sorry condition of the evening before.

'As you know, Watson, my knowledge of the geography of our beloved city is second to none, so I immediately made for a sector of the East End where I knew a large number of small shops and business premises plied their trade. My research at these establishments revealed two key facts that have since proved to be invaluable. First, I was soon made to realise that the threat posed to these proprietors was very real and that it ran deep. Everyone that I spoke to expressed a grave fear of even discussing these matters with me; much less providing me with any tangible assistance.

'Second, I very soon realised that the radius of Wilson's influence was far wider than anything that I could previously have imagined. Watson, your dramatic and vivid description of his being 'the black plague' is not so far from the truth. However, this realisation also helped me with my task, because I knew of a small tinker's workshop that is located on the very fringes of Wilson's self-imposed boundaries.

'As you can imagine, I made for this workshop without a moment's delay and I soon arrived on the doorstep of Jacob Dobson, an elderly gentleman with grey sparkling eyes and the heart of a lion. He greeted me with a broad toothless smile and a mug of tea that proved to be as tepid as it had been toxic.

'Once I had recovered from my first and only sip of that noxious brew, I explained to Mr Dobson the intention behind my visit. He was surprisingly agreeable to my scheme and it was soon agreed that I should stand in his stead that very evening, when Wilson's men were due to arrive for their regular payment. He entrusted me with his keys and I advised him to remain as far away from his workshop as possible for the next forty-eight hours.

'I settled myself down for a long and thankless evening with my only companion, a liberal supply of my old shag. A battered carriage clock, cloaked in a thick layer of metal dusk, told me of the slow progress of the evening, but all inclinations for sleep were stifled by the rush of expectation that ran through me.

'That feeling was heightened when the old timepiece chimed out the news that it was now eleven o'clock at night: the appointed time of arrival for Wilson's henchmen. A loud single rap upon the back door had alerted me to their punctuality and I stood up slowly and gingerly in order that I attain the movements of my assumed characterisation.

'Watson, you can imagine their surprise upon finding me standing there, instead of their intended victim, when I did eventually open the door. I received an almighty shove against the wall as they burst in. They immediately demanded to know the whereabouts of "the other gentleman."

'I explained that "my cousin" had been taken poorly and that he had asked me to meet with them in his stead. To this substitution they did not raise a single word of objection. However, it was a different matter when their demands for payment were met by an empty hand and an abject refusal to pay.

'I told them that the funds would not be available until the following evening and that if it had been up to me, there would have been no payment forthcoming whatsoever! The results of my lack of funds and those words of bravado were somewhat more painful than I could have anticipated, and I was left lying there in the condition in which you found me.'

'Good heavens, Holmes!' I protested. 'Do you have absolutely no regard for your own well-being?'

'What other recourse did I have?' Holmes implored. 'After all, in order that I maintain the integrity of my assumed identity, I could hardly resist or fight back. Although in truth, even should I have not been in character, any resistance on my part, against such large and formidable foes, would undoubtedly have had the same dire and painful outcome.

'I was left in little doubt as to the consequences of any further refusal to pay, when these jovial gentlemen dismantled poor Dobson's rear door with just a few blows from their enormous boots! I was also threatened with the honour of meeting Wilson himself on the occasion of their next visit to Dobson's, at midnight tonight.'

'But Holmes, that is barely twelve hours from now!'

'Exactly, Watson. I really must get that wire off to Inspector Lestrade without a second's delay! Mrs Hudson!'

As soon as our harassed landlady had bustled off with Holmes's message, my friend requested a full nine hours of quiet and complete rest. As both his friend and doctor, I wholeheartedly approved of that at least.

* * *

At precisely nine o'clock on that same evening, Holmes finally emerged from his room dressed in his overcoat and hat while brandishing his weight-loaded cane. His transformation into the elderly tinker had once again been a remarkable one and his cheery laugh showed me that he viewed our impending adventure with an unjustifiable relish. I touched the revolver which sat securely and reassuringly in my coat pocket.

We were greeted at the street door by our old friend and ally, the cabby, Dave 'Gunner' King, who sped us along to the same address with which Holmes had already furnished Inspector Lestrade, one among a labyrinth of small side streets that run behind Petticoat Lane. King steered his cab along a narrow, muddy and uneven alleyway that led us to the rear of Dobson's workshop, our point of rendezvous, before ensuring that he and his vehicle remained out of sight until next called upon.

The damage caused to the door by Holmes's assailants was obvious, although Holmes himself had subsequently arranged for a makeshift repair, to ensure the security of Dobson's premises in his absence.

We synchronised our timepieces and realised that our early arrival gave us the opportunity for a cigarette or two before taking up our positions. Holmes led Lestrade and I to a dusty screen behind which we could remain out of sight, although a jagged tear down its centre afforded us a clear view of the remnants of the back door, as Holmes had anticipated.

Once Holmes was satisfied with his arrangements, he allowed one of Lestrade's constables to enter with Mr Dobson, who had been securely escorted from his temporary bolthole in time to meet his irrevocable appointment. The genial old man seemed to be surprisingly underwhelmed by the dramatic events that were soon to unfold before him and he was attentive to every letter of Holmes's detailed instructions.

My friends' attention to detail was most admirable, and he even counted and then recounted the amount of money that Dobson had brought with him, to ensure that the old man's safety should not be jeopardised by a simple miscalculation. He thought it to be more natural for Dobson to be working on repairs to his backdoor, at the time of Wilson's arrival, than have him wait nervously in the dark. Holmes lit a lantern at the rear of the workshop to better aid him in this, and also to ensure that Lestrade had a clear view of all that was soon to transpire. Dobson dutifully set to his task while Holmes positioned two more of Lestrade's men in a shadowy doorway on the opposite side of the alley.

By now, the time had crept along to five minutes before midnight and satisfied with his preparations, Holmes crept over to his position deep within the shadows of the workshop. Then we waited.

Wilson and his men were agonisingly late and the chimes of midnight were more strident as a consequence of our strained apprehension. Had it not been for the constant tapping of Dobson's hammer upon his door, the silence that followed would have been excruciating. As it was, we all held our stoic stillness and the hands on the old clock seemed to have ground to a halt.

We all hoped that Dobson would keep his nerve and continue with his work, for he had begun to glance anxiously over his shoulder towards Holmes's position, as the hour progressed. Finally, at the very moment when I feared that our game was surely up, we were rewarded by the sound of three sets of boots walking slowly and deliberately along the alleyway towards where we were laying in wait.

Dobson continued bravely with his work, right up to the moment that the three shadows appeared in the doorway. Two of the shadows were pretty much as

I had imagined them to be, tall, hulking and ungainly. The third, however, remained indeterminate until it came within the pale glow of the tiny lantern.

The larger shadows stood at the doorway, but the sight of the third caused in me an involuntary shudder. Never before had I been witness to the very epitome of pure evil. The figure was short and slight, dressed impeccably in a fine mohair coat, a lustrous top hat and a pair of shoes that positively shone, despite the dismal illumination. It says much of a man's nature, however, when he attaches far more importance to his outward appearance than he does to his inner sanctity.

Even from my current distance, the stench that wafted from this most disreputable of men was overpowering. His unwashed face and hair were obvious signs of his lack of self-respect and indicative of his priorities. However, it was when he broke into a sinister smile that his true nature became manifest. His teeth were black, uneven and sparse. His eyes were dark and lifeless and when he spoke his thin ulcerated lips seeped blood. His voice was surprisingly deep and guttural.

'Ah, Mr Dobson, I am glad to see that you are well again and that you have removed your idiotic cousin from our little business transaction.' Wilson's voice suddenly rose to a hellish shriek. 'He was lucky to have escaped with his life, and so are you!'

Dobson dropped his hammer and took several steps back, so shocked was he by Wilson's screech, but he held his nerve, knowing full well that we could not yet make our move.

'Let me now make matters as clear to you as I possibly can, Mr Dobson, in order that there should be no future ambiguity or misunderstanding between the two of us, of course,' Wilson continued in his higher octave.

'You should be glad to know that the arrangements between us will continue exactly as before. There shall be no punishment levied, despite your unforgivable behaviour. However, should you ever try to trick me again, I assure you that your life will never be the same. My colleagues outside are more than capable of levelling this place to the ground with just a few well-placed blows. Even were you able to return your trade to its nomadic roots, I am sure that your skills would be harder to employ were you to be without both of your hands!' The pitch of Wilson's voice reached a crescendo. Mercifully, Dobson maintained his silence.

Wilson clicked his fingers and the two lumbering forms moved forward and through the doorway. He laughed manically and then held his palm out towards the quivering Dobson.

'So, Mr Dobson, as you have probably realised, it is now time for you to hand over my money.' Our vigilance had been rewarded at last and I sensed Lestrade's hand move slowly towards his revolver, an action that mirrored my own.

Each man was ready to pounce at a moment's notice and we were attentive to every movement within the workshop. As Dobson's money passed slowly from hand to hand, Lestrade signalled his men with a short blast from his whistle and they were across the alley in an instant.

Wilson's curses were violent and unrepeatable and he wrapped his right hand around Dobson's throat with a manic delight.

'One more move from any one of you and I assure you that I will not hesitate for an instant in choking the life out of this imbecile!' Wilson declared, and there was not one of us who did not believe him.

We all stood our ground and replaced our guns, but at that moment a scuffle that had ensued outside between the constables and one of Wilson's henchmen, exploded unexpectedly into the workshop. One of the constables was hurled through the shattered doorway and collided violently with Wilson's legs. His grip on Dobson's neck was immediately released and we moved towards him with our guns at the ready.

One of Wilson's men was stupid enough to rush towards us and Lestrade brought him down with a single shot. The other made a bolt for it down the alley, but with both constables in immediate pursuit, the result of this chase was inevitable, not least because King had pulled up his cab at the opposite end of the alley, thereby barring the ruffian's escape.

Wilson's resistance was over and he held up his clasped hands in anticipation of Lestrade's handcuffs. The inspector did not hesitate for a second in applying them.

'Well, well!' Wilson cackled. 'If it isn't my old adversary Inspector Lestrade! You have finally undone me, but not without a little help, I fancy, eh?' Wilson jerked his head towards a movement in the shadows and my friend finally made himself known. 'I should have known that you were neither brave enough nor intelligent enough to have devised this scheme for yourself. I congratulate you, Mr Sherlock Holmes!'

'I have never felt less deserving of congratulations, I assure you. There is no less noble a task than bringing down a creature such as you.' Holmes turned on his heels as Wilson was led away.

'It is a waste of time, Mr Holmes; you must already know that I shall be back before very long.'

'I think you will find that we have more than enough reliable and willing witnesses on this occasion. I will see to it that you shall never see the light of day again,' Holmes declared with a dismissive wave of his hand.

As the hapless Wilson was dragged unceremoniously from the room, Lestrade walked towards Holmes with an outstretched hand.

'Thank you, Mr Holmes,' he said simply, as the two men shook hands. 'This time you have risked much in your pursuit of justice and, in doing so, you have eliminated a dark entity from our streets once and for all.'

Wilson had clearly overheard Lestrade's words of congratulations and his voice echoed back down the alleyway towards us.

'Do not be so sure of yourselves! I know the ways of the Brotherhood!' His ghastly voice slowly faded into the shadows, but the words left us with a feeling of great unease.

The effects of the last few days finally took their toll on my friend and once Lestrade had left, Holmes let out a deep sigh as he leaned against the dank wall for support. Fortunately, King's cab pulled up outside at that very moment and between us we helped Holmes climb aboard.

The journey back to Baker Street was completed in silence and Holmes was asleep within an instant. However, it was gratifying to observe that he had fallen into unconsciousness with a smile of satisfaction upon his wounded and sallow face.

It was only now, on the eve of my momentous journey, that I understood the true significance of Wilson's parting words.

CHAPTER TWO

REFLECTIONS ON A TRAIN

To a lonely and solitary traveller, a long train journey can be a most hypnotic, therapeutic, and illuminating experience.

It is an opportunity for reflection, contemplation and, in my case, recollection. The gentle sway of the carriage, the rhythmic pulsations of the engine as it spews out its grey and toxic steam, even the alterations in the timing of the wheels upon the track, caused by their passage over the points, produces a most beneficial and meditative effect.

As any student of rail travel will readily attest to, the sixteen-hour stretch of rail between Brussels and Munich is undoubtedly the longest leg of any journey from London to the Bavarian capital, and therefore affords the traveller more than enough time to reconcile and collate his thoughts.

There can be little doubt in the minds of anyone who has read the accounts of my adventures in Rome and Egypt[2] in the company of my good friend Sherlock Holmes, and the subsequent gamut of crimes with which we had been

---

[2]   From 'Sherlock Holmes and the Unholy Trinity' by P.D.G.

bombarded upon our return, that this was an exercise of which I was in the direst need!

Not for the first time during the course of my long and exhilarating association with the world's only unofficial consulting detective had my head and thoughts been left befuddled by a succession of dramatic events that were, at times, beyond my comprehension. Therefore, I took full advantage of this long and lonely passage and tried to make sense of my reasons for actually being on board this train in the first place.

Our interest and involvement with the 'Unholy Trinity'[3] and the associated Bavarian Brotherhood had begun six long months ago, and at our very own breakfast table. An imposing and rather threatening Bedouin had warned us to stay well clear of the affairs of his people and, to demonstrate his intent, he had left a chair and the door to our rooms irreparably damaged.

Within moments of the Bedouin's departure, a wire arrived which requested Holmes's immediate attendance in the Vatican City to investigate the mysterious death of the Pope's assumed successor, Cardinal Tosca. Understandably, the opportunity of serving His Holiness and working alongside our old friend, Inspector Gialli,[4] once again, was one that proved to be irresistible to my friend. Consequently, we departed for the Eternal City on the first available train.

Little did we realise that this intriguing murder investigation was going to lead us upon the trail of a missing Coptic Gospel and the ruthless organisation that had been determined to achieve its possession. A potentially murderous attack upon Gialli led us to the conclusion that our next destination should be an ancient Coptic church in the land of Egypt.

During our time in Egypt we were privileged to meet a number of fascinating characters, not the least of them being

---

[3]   From 'Sherlock Holmes and the Unholy Trinity' by P.D.G.

[4]   From 'The Adventure of the Dying Gaul – *The Lost Files of Sherlock Holmes* by P.D.G.

Shenouda, a Coptic priest who appeared to be as ancient as the very church in which he served! During the course of a long and uncomfortable night, Shenouda explained the nature and significance of the obscure Gospel of Mary Magdalene.

Holmes's examination of the rooms of Hashmoukh, a dubious purveyor of objects and manuscripts of antiquity, revealed a link between Hashmoukh's brutal murder, Mary's gospel, and the shadowy Professor Ronald Sydney.

We were surprised to discover that our Bedouin visitor also served as the guardian of Shenouda's church. Despite its dramatic nature, his had been a friendly warning and this had been confirmed when he saved us from near certain death at the hands of two marauding horsemen on the platform of the station at Alexandria.

Our return visit to Rome proved to be somewhat briefer than the first. We were gratified to note that Gialli was well on the road to recovery and Holmes took great pleasure in placing the name of Tosca's murderer into his eager hands, while deferring any credit that might have been due to him.

Our adventures even continued on the way back to London, and resulted in the apprehension of Gialli's assailants as we approached the terminus of Paris. Once back at Baker Street, our old friend, Inspector Lestrade, presented Holmes with the type of subtle and intriguing little problem on which he normally thrived.

However, on this rare occasion it was I who had discovered the truth upon a mortician's table, although Holmes soon formulated a link between this murder and the problem at hand: the Bavarian Brotherhood. The murder victim Christophe Decaux, the doctor who had falsified his coroner's report, the lawyer who had arranged the extradition of Gialli's assailants, and Professor Sydney himself, all proved to be members of the Diogenes Club!

No doubt wishing to remove such elements from his club, Mycroft, Holmes's elder brother, had arranged the release of Sydney's henchman that Holmes might follow them to his lair. The ensuing confrontation was of such a violent nature that it was only Holmes and I who had emerged unscathed; although, thankfully, Lestrade's injuries proved to be only superficial.

We returned to Baker Street drained of both energy and emotion. Holmes's deflation was compounded by the news from his friend Elraji, of the Cairo police department, that Shenouda had been found brutally slain. The scale and ruthlessness of the Bavarian Brotherhood was now beyond doubt, particularly when it emerged that Decaux's murderer, Roger Ashley, had also been a member of the Diogenes Club.

Holmes was convinced that the 'Unholy Trinity' was comprised of Cardinal Pietro, the colleague and murderer of Cardinal Tosca and the late Professor Sydney. With Pietro now exiled to a distant mission in the depths of Africa, the only potential threat seemed to reside with the third and, as yet unidentified, member of the Trinity.

* * *

At this juncture I had decided to sample the wares of the buffet car. However, my previous experience of such eateries resulted in my approaching my allocated table with a degree of trepidation. Mercifully, the meal that I had been presented with proved to be more than adequate and with my hunger now satiated, I made my way towards the observation car, where I smoked a rather fine cigar.

I noticed that the further east we travelled, the more prevalent became the frost and ice that one might have expected to see at that time of year. The shimmering white glow of the moon outlined and highlighted the spectacular scenery that now surrounded us and the distant mountains began to reveal their shadowy and menacing forms.

With a shiver, I pulled up my jacket lapel, hurriedly completed my smoke, and then made my way back to my compartment with a large and warming glass of cognac, there to reflect upon the recent chain of events that had led to my taking this journey.

There had been no time for Holmes and I to dwell upon the identity of that third member of the Trinity, for we were immediately plunged headlong into a maelstrom of new and intriguing cases, the sheer volume of which had been unprecedented throughout our association.

The peculiar persecution of John Vincent Harden[5] had been a matter that had begun rather inauspiciously, for our client departed from our rooms in a premature rage the moment that Holmes had accused him of being rather more than frugal with the truth. However, our subsequent investigations vindicated Holmes's assertions. Our discoveries led us to the disturbing conclusion that Harden had been a member of the Diogenes Club and the reasons for his frequent visits to West Hampstead had had nothing to do with his accountants at all, as he had asserted. In fact, he had been enjoying the company of a young actress, Sophie Sinclair, and without the knowledge of his wife.

Nevertheless, our plans were soon scuppered when, the following morning, the papers greeted us with the news that Harden had met with a horrendous death, under the wheels of a train at West Hampstead station! Inspector Lestrade was convinced that Harden's wife and another, younger, woman had caused his death.

With his usual mental dexterity, Holmes lost no time in disproving Lestrade's theory and the disgruntled inspector accepted his defeat after a brief conversation with the elusive actress. Although the conclusion to this case had not been entirely satisfactory, it had at least afforded me the opportunity of meeting Miss Sinclair, a beautiful and accomplished young lady who had ignited in me a feeling that I had not experienced since first meeting my late wife, Mary.[6]

---

5   From 'The Four-Handed Game' by P.D.G.
6   Mary Morstan from 'The Sign of Four' by Sir A.C.D.

It was on the following morning that the floodgates had been truly opened. Upon returning from an early morning walk, I had been surprised to find that Holmes was not only awake and dressed, but that he was already engaged in consultation with our latest client, the historian and translator, Mr Denbigh Grey.

Grey had been employed to translate a manuscript that detailed the military campaigns of Alexander the Great. Notwithstanding the misgivings that Grey had harboured initially, it had been a task that he had found to be too intriguing to refuse. Furthermore, his new employer sounded like a man who was not accustomed to being rejected.

Grey had not only been greatly troubled by his employer's threatening manner, but also by the presence of a number of obvious and inexplicable anomalies within the text. At once Holmes had concluded that the irregularities constituted a subtle and ingenious form of code or cipher, and he had rubbed his hands together excitedly at the prospect of undertaking the considerable challenge of deciphering it.

Nevertheless, I had felt duty bound to remonstrate with him, once he had offhandedly dismissed our new client, for I was certain that he had also recognised the identity of Grey's employer from his most singular and detailed description. It was none other than our old adversary, Theodore Daxer, the Austrian spy.[7]

However, when I pointed this out to him, I soon realised that Holmes had been totally oblivious to my presence. He had brought out his blackboard and chalk, and he was immediately absorbed in the irresistible task of solving the riddle. He was rudely interrupted by the agitated form of Inspector Bradstreet. Under a different set of circumstances, Holmes would have jumped at the opportunity of helping Bradstreet with his predicament, for he had been investigating

---

[7] From 'The Dundas Separation Case' – *The Annals of Sherlock Holmes* by P.D.G.

nothing less than the theft of a solid gold mandolin from the Bloomsbury museum. This time, however, Bradstreet had to be at his most persuasive before Holmes would even agree to listen to him, much less visit the scene of the crime. Nevertheless, Bradstreet departed buoyed by the thought of having Holmes by his side once more, and my friend immediately despatched a wire to Menachem Goldman, an unquestionable authority on stolen jewellery, who went about his nefarious trade under the guise of a harmless Polish Jew.

Once I had concluded that I would receive neither a word nor even an acknowledgement from Holmes in the foreseeable future, I decided to clear my head with a brisk walk. I soon found myself outside the Garrick Theatre and before long I was in the queue for tickets for the matinee performance of *Macbeth*, which I knew featured Sophie Sinclair in the minor, albeit tragically dramatic role of Lady Macduff.

However, the real-life events, which immediately followed the slaughter of Lady Macduff and her household, were equally remarkable, though thankfully with less fatal consequences.

A hush had descended upon the stage at the moment of Lady Macduff's demise, and the entire cast had crowded around the still and bloody form of Sophie Sinclair. I was up on to the stage in an instant and I had assumed temporary control of the situation, prior to the arrival of the authorities. They appeared promptly in the form of Inspector Lestrade and his men from Scotland Yard.

Miss Sinclair survived the attack and once she had been taken into medical care, Lestrade began to interview the remainder of the cast, while his men and I instigated a systematic search of the theatre.

We soon realised that one of the extras had not been accounted for, and while I had been exploring one of a myriad of corridors, I had been set upon by someone masquerading as one of Lestrade's constables! Lestrade's man was subsequently discovered within a costume basket and I eventually returned to consciousness once back within our rooms in Baker Street.

I was surprised by the sight of my friend peering anxiously down at me, but it was not long before he felt ready to advise me of recent events. His examination of the museum's vault had revealed the presence of two guards who had only recently been employed by the late Professor Sydney, and they had undoubtedly been the perpetrators of the theft. Furthermore, an interview with Inspector Lestrade, which took place during my extended period of unconsciousness, revealed that his description of Miss Sinclair's probable assailant matched exactly that of the museum guard who had managed to slip through the net of Scotland Yard. I now pondered my theory of a vast conspiracy emanating from the Diogenes Club and I would have proposed this to Holmes had we not been interrupted by the arrival of Goldman, in his guise of a Polish Rabbi.

A brief interview, which revealed that Goldman's knowledge of the mandolin had far exceeded that of both Holmes and the police, concluded with Goldman accepting Holmes's commission with a promise of results within twenty-four hours!

Having dismissed my theories with a patronising smile, Holmes told me that he remained convinced that the key lay within the mysteries of Daxer's code. He sat down despondently with his pipe as he grudgingly admitted to me that he was no closer to breaking the code than he had been at the outset of his work.

However, the news that we were to receive from a nervous young constable early the following morning did much to alter my friend's opinion of my theories, and even induced that rarity, an apology from Sherlock Holmes!

Holmes's association with Langdale Pike[8] had never been one that I had ever fully understood, nor endorsed.

---

8   From 'The Adventure of the Three Gables' by Sir A.C.D.

Pike had plied a nefarious trade within the gossip columns of those newspapers favoured by society. Many a time would his poisonous tittle-tattle break the hearts and shatter the dreams of an illustrious family. Yet Holmes seemed to absolve Pike of all guilt by forming an exchange of information with him, whenever it might furnish him with a clue.

Nevertheless, the news of Pike's death — his throat had been savagely severed from ear to ear at his club in St James's Street — shook both Holmes and I to the core. Holmes fell back into his chair as an awful realisation came upon him. With a deep sigh of resignation, he despatched two mysterious wires before we set off to begin our investigations at St James' Street.

Holmes's examination of Pike's private room had revealed very little, there was only a scrawled note on his desk, which Holmes managed to salvage without being seen. Holmes also found it curious that Inspector Gregson had left the scene of the crime before the conclusion of his investigations. Upon our return to Baker Street, we had been confronted by the sight of two very irritated detectives on the point of breaking their appointment.

Holmes excused our late arrival, and I realised at once that Inspectors Bradstreet and Lestrade had been the recipients of Holmes's hurriedly despatched wires. During a solemn enrolment ceremony, Holmes outlined the gravity and significance of the events that had involved each of us during the past few weeks.

He invited them both to join us in playing a dangerous four-handed game, but when Holmes became distracted by the arrival of another anomaly from Denbigh Grey, it fell to me to explain the connection between recent events, the Diogenes Club, and the Bavarian Brotherhood.

Holmes turned back from his blackboard to apologise for having removed the note from Pike's desk; however, he was as confused as the rest of us at the eclectic nature of the names upon it. Although Adele Fox and Austin-Simons had both been familiar to us, their association with each other was somewhat less than obvious.

Miss Fox had been Sophie Sinclair's friend and confidante, while Austin-Simons had been the lawyer responsible for the extradition of Sydney's henchman. Their connection to each other would be forged in a most dramatic fashion, on the morning following the funeral of Langdale Pike.

I awoke to find that the newspapers and the teeming streets were resonating with the news of a ritual slaying upon the steps of St Mary's Church, Whitechapel, and that the victim had been none other than the tragic Adele Fox. The mutilation visited upon her had been an exact duplication of that performed upon the final victim of Jack the Ripper: Mary Kelly.

Although the motive for Miss Fox's death had been obvious to Holmes, that was her tenuous connection to John Vincent Harden, the reason for such a public display of their ruthless efficiency, had been somewhat less so. Holmes was now convinced that each crime was being deliberately designed to lure him on to a preordained path, and he had no intention of disappointing its architects.

We were greeted upon the steps of St Mary's by Inspector Gregson, who now appeared to have been embarrassed by the dark cloud that had been hanging over him. His initial uncooperative manner altered as soon as he realised that Holmes was not oblivious to his deliberate negligence at the scene of Langdale Pike's murder.

Gregson's reward for his obvious display of collaboration had been nothing less than an attempt upon his life from a long-range rifle. Once I had satisfied myself that Gregson's life was in no immediate danger, I joined Holmes in his pursuit of the inspector's would-be assassin.

The site of the church had been secured by a tight cordon of police officers, so we soon flushed out the marksman. The exchange of gunfire that ensued resulted in my bringing the fellow down with a shot from my revolver. I could scarcely believe my ears when Holmes berated me for having deprived him of a potential font of information, in the lifeless form of Austin-Simons!

Holmes's appreciation soon superseded his annoyance and before long we found ourselves outside the offices of Police Commissioner, Sir Edward Bradford. Holmes had been excluded from the original 'Ripper' investigations, for reasons that would shortly become apparent, but we soon discovered that Bradford had been cut from an entirely different cloth to that of his predecessor, Sir Charles Warren. Significantly, Bradford had no association with the Diogenes Club.

Far from being obstructive and uncooperative, the genial Commissioner actually went out of his way to facilitate our investigations in every conceivable manner. He placed his driver at my disposal that I might examine the sorry remains of Miss Fox at the Whitechapel mortuary, and he even allowed Holmes access to the highly classified files from the original investigations of 1888.

Despite my having witnessed every aspect of Holmes's amazing powers of deduction, it was true to say that he had never lost the ability to surprise me. Therefore, upon my return to Bradford's office, my astonishment upon hearing of his discoveries and conclusions can be well understood.

Not only had my friend identified Miss Fox's murderer, but he had soon convinced Bradford and I that this individual had also previously gone by the name of Jack the Ripper! Because of the circumstantial nature of Holmes's evidence, Bradford could not instigate an arrest. However, he assured us that Dr Marcus Harding, who had also falsified Decaux's autopsy, would be struck off immediately and that Bradford's department would work tirelessly in corroborating Holmes's conclusions.

Upon our return to Baker Street, Holmes and I were greeted by a raft of new and exciting evidence. Denbigh Grey had been so intent on presenting his latest discovery, with the intention of bringing the matter to a speedy conclusion, that he had thrown caution to the wind by delivering it to us in person.

Holmes had been visibly motivated by this new anomaly and on this occasion, he forsook his blackboard for his notebook. Once he had despatched his customary wires, he questioned Grey as to the exact circumstances of his liaisons with Theodore Daxer. It was clearly now the time for Holmes to flush out his quarry and he dismissed Grey with a dire warning, but also a promise that his predicament would soon be resolved.

Our next visitor's piece of news was no less dramatic than his startling change in appearance. Menachem Goldman had exchanged his Polish Rabbi persona in favour of that of a clean-shaven and dapper English gentleman, but his explanation for such a transformation was a cause of great concern.

His inquiries into the matter of the Venetian mandolin had led him along a path that he had clearly not anticipated. His usual contacts held their silence in fear of their lives. The scant knowledge that he had been able to glean, revealed an organisation of a size and scale that he had never encountered before.

Nevertheless, Goldman had managed to trace the mandolin to a remote castle in Bavaria which had been constructed for the reclusive King Ludwig II some thirty years earlier. Abandoned upon the premature death of this taciturn ruler, Neuschwanstein Castle was now in the occupancy of another recluse, a man shrouded in mystery and a black silk head mask that was never removed while he was under public gaze.

Holmes's normally taut nerves were stretched to their limits and he did not relax again until he had arranged a rendezvous for the following evening with both Inspectors Bradstreet and Lestrade. He advised them to be fully armed and I was now in little doubt that a small note, which Holmes had slipped to Denbigh Grey, was his means of setting a trap for Theodore Daxer.

We arrived at the abandoned house in Park Street well ahead of the appointed time and were able to position ourselves inconspicuously, long before the arrival of our prey. The vigil proved to be a long and unnerving one, and the traumatic silence was only broken once we heard the street door below closing behind our quarry and a familiar Germanic voice call for Denbigh Grey to show himself.

Daxer had not been alone, but his confederate, a notorious assassin named Carl Irwin, did not possess his colleague's steely nerves. The ensuing melee resulted in an injury to Lestrade, a bullet in the thigh for Irwin — which subsequently proved to be a fatal one — and Holmes diving down the stairs in urgent pursuit of Theodore Daxer.

The chase proved to be a short one. The awful sound of collision reverberated up the stairs and I arrived on street level in time to hear Daxer's vile and final curses. The Austrian spy had been crushed beneath the wheels of an onrushing horse-drawn omnibus, but Holmes appeared to be rather more affected by Daxer's thinly veiled threat to the life of his brother, Mycroft.

Holmes's initial reaction transformed into anxiety when, on the following day, Mycroft could neither be found at his lodgings nor at his office. Our questioning at both establishments revealed neither a hint nor a clue as to his whereabouts, but for a man of such singular regularity to have deviated from his daily itinerary was more astonishing than if he had been an ordinary person.

Holmes had been clearly disturbed by his brother's behaviour and his air of despondency indicated to me that he now feared for Mycroft's life. Upon our return to Baker Street, he sank into his chair with listless despair, and his pipe, hanging upon the edge of his lower lip, remained unlit.

He was not aroused by the news of Lestrade's return to duty, following his recovery from injury, nor was he particularly overjoyed upon hearing of Sophie Sinclair's release from hospital. However, he was surprisingly insistent that I should visit her in West Hampstead, without a moment's delay.

At first I was suspicious of his motives; after all, I did not intend to be duped by him again, as I had been once before at Meiringen.[9] He had convinced me that his intention was that I warn her of the danger that she still faced.

The look upon Mrs Hudson's face, upon my return, alerted me to the fact that my worst fears had been realised. Not only had Holmes made a sudden departure with his small overnight bag, but he had also taken three unusual precautions while on his way to the door. Individually they had been indicative, but collectively they were conclusive. Sherlock Holmes had absolutely no intention of my being able to follow him!

I could not help a wry smile as I contemplated his thought process. According to Mrs Hudson, he became animated once more upon receiving two wires that he had been expecting from his colleagues in Bavaria.

Once read, these wires were hurled on to the fire and he would not turn away until he had been assured of their complete incineration. He had been just as thorough in his obliteration of every chalk mark on his blackboard, and when he had asked our landlady to find him a cab, he insisted that it should not be our old friend King!

I decided to use my friend's method in calculating his intended destination. The wires had probably told him that Mycroft had already been sighted in Bavaria. I had been in little doubt that it had been Mycroft who had initiated the early release of Roger Ashley; undoubtedly that Ashley might lead him to the retreat of his powerful confederate.

I sought the secret of Holmes's blackboard from Denbigh Grey, and I was astonished to note the name that the first letter of each anomaly composed: G R U N E R! Baron Gruner,[10] otherwise known as the Austrian murderer, had been one of Holmes's most insidious and dangerous opponents, and he had sworn a terrible vengeance after he had been hideously scarred by the hand of our vengeful client.

---

[9] From 'The Adventure of the Final Problem' by Sir A.C.D.
[10] From 'The Adventure of the Illustrious Client' by Sir A.C.D.

It all fitted together! Goldman had traced the mandolin to a remote castle in Bavaria, occupied by a recluse in a black silk mask, anxious to disguise his hideous deformity. Using a vast network of agents and employing an array of intriguing crimes, Gruner had succeeded in luring both of the Holmes brothers to a potentially deadly fate.

As if I had needed any further confirmation, and despite Holmes's imprudent precaution, I felt certain that 'Gunner' King would have been able to trace the cabbie employed by Holmes. This had been the final link in my chain, and now I awaited confirmation from Holmes himself that my proposed journey should not prove to be in vain.

Apropos of the traumas that his three-year hiatus had caused me to endure, surely Holmes could not treat me so shabbily again? Finally, on the third day, I found his message in the agony columns of the *Telegraph*. Both Holmes brothers were alive and safe in each other's company. The message had been signed by Sigurdsson, the persona that Holmes had adopted during his extensive travels.

My resolution now was to hasten to their location before their current state of affairs had a chance to change for the worse.

CHAPTER THREE

THE CASTLE OF NEUSCHWANSTEIN

Naturally enough, 'Gunner' King required considerable persuasion before he would even consider divulging his information. After all, Sherlock Holmes is not a man that many would dare to betray, even should an opportunity for doing so present itself, as I had once discovered to my cost. Nevertheless, once I had presented the cabby with the potential and dire consequences of my not reaching the Holmes brothers in time, he finally acquiesced.

King's colleague, Tom Ford, was frustratingly difficult to locate, even for him. There were various public houses that he frequented, when not at his cab, and King obligingly helped me eliminate each of them, one by one. Finally, at a justifiably notorious establishment known as The White Hart, we found our quarry, mercifully at the point of his indulgence whereby he was still capable of cohesive thought and some form of comprehensible communication.

Initially Ford had been reluctant to desert the warmth of such convivial company and the hearth of the interior for the chill night air and the badgering of a stranger. However, once I had pressed a coin into his lacerated palm and King had offered him the support of his broad shoulders, Ford began to move uncertainly towards the door.

Once King had assured him of the validity and sincerity of my intentions, Ford soon advised me of Holmes's travel plans. Apparently, Holmes had booked himself aboard an early morning boat train from Victoria bound for Paris, and a quick consultation with my trusty Bradshaw's indicated the time of the train that would best connect me with one leaving the French capital for Brussels.

Logistically, this made little sense to me, as there would certainly have been a more direct route available to him. However, I was certain that this had been yet another of Holmes's attempts at throwing me off his track, but I decided to follow in his wake meticulously, for fear of his plan actually working.

Satisfied with the arrangements that I had now put into place, I hurried back to Baker Street to pack a small bag and to inform Mrs Hudson of my intentions. Obviously, I omitted those details that might have caused her too much unnecessary concern, but this did not prevent her nervous disposition from coming to the fore. I tried my best at consoling her and eventually I was even able to persuade her to prepare for me a light packed lunch for the first part of my journey.

Inevitably, I spent a restless last night in Baker Street. My exhausted mind had been ceaselessly analysing every potential outcome of my venture. I must confess that not one of these had culminated in a positive result and that by the morning I was almost resolved to abandoning the enterprise altogether.

Notwithstanding these misgivings of mine when, at the appointed time, King arrived to whisk me back to Victoria station, I climbed aboard his cab without a moment's hesitation. With not a little nervous tension, I finally launched my crusade with resolution.

The journey from Paris to Brussels did not present me with any great difficulty and I connected with the train to Munich with precision. I spent the sixteen-hour journey from the Belgian capital to Munich in the manner that I have previously described, and I concluded this phase of my journey with renewed optimism.

However, a brief delay caused by an unscheduled stop for fuel caused me to miss the next link in my vehicular chain, and I was forced to spend an unsolicited overnight stay in the Bavarian capital. The lateness of the hour, and therefore the desperate nature of my situation, afforded me little choice in the way of accommodation. Consequently, I was forced to spend a cold and uncomfortable night in a sparse and unheated room.

It goes without saying that such an awful establishment had little to offer me in the way of a decent breakfast, so my relief at finding myself aboard a warm carriage on my way to Fussen, my next port of call, might be well understood. Although smaller and slower than the previous trains on my journey, it had made a comfortable and steady progress throughout the eighty-two miles that we had still to traverse.

All the while the distant mountains began to loom increasingly larger, and the rapidly decreasing temperatures were made more obvious by the amount of ice that adorned those lofty and ominous peaks. I shuddered at the sight and was extremely grateful for the small whisky flask in my inside pocket.

I steeled my resolve to complete this uncomfortable journey with the thought of the potential dangers that my friend and his brother might even now be facing. My memories of Baron Gruner did little to comfort me either. Although the case of *The Adventure of the Illustrious Client* had been finally resolved by the determined actions of one of our clients, it is also true to say that the retributions taken out on Holmes by two of Gruner's henchman resulted in a set of injuries the like of which I should never like to gaze upon again.

The fictitious story, with which we supplied some of the more popular newspapers, recounting how perilously close to death my friend had been after this cowardly attack, had not been as far from the truth as Holmes would have led me to believe. Furthermore, the unsubstantiated stories of how Gruner had murdered his own wife, together with the young shepherd boy who had supposedly witnessed this heinous crime, did little to alleviate my anxiety.

Consequently, as the train slowly pulled into the single platform of the tiny station of Fussen, my jaw was set firm and I was determined to carry out whatever deeds and face any danger that might lie ahead of me. I was surprised and somewhat frustrated, therefore, to note that the town of Fussen was rather larger than I had anticipated.

This picturesque town had been established upon the banks of the River Lech and it boasted an abbey, a medieval square, and a flourishing violin and lute manufacturing industry. Obviously, these attractions were of very little interest to me at the time, primarily because the size of the place undoubtedly rendered the next stage of my search all the more difficult.

My worst fears were soon realised when my enquiries at the station, and then at some of Fussen's most notable establishments, drew unanimously negative responses. It was almost as if Holmes and Mycroft had never set foot in the place. After all, it was not as if either of their descriptions was anything less than most singular. Yet my questioning yielded nothing more than a series of solemn and nonplussed shaking of heads.

After a while my search became aimless and despondent, and before long I found myself back at the station, convinced that my quest was condemned to failure. By this time, I had become both cold and hungry, and, mercifully, I noticed a small medieval *gasthof*, The Kroner, a nondescript establishment that must have escaped my attention when I had first arrived. Initially my only intention had been to feed and warm myself there, something that I was well able to do with their excellent schnitzel and some heated mead.

However, as I was taking my leave, I noticed an elderly gentleman who I had recognised from one of my earlier places of inquiry. To my great excitement and joy he had recognised my description of Holmes at once, and before long he was leading me towards a small stable situated on the outskirts of the town.

Here he had introduced me to Peter Kohl the younger, which had amused me for he could not have been a day younger than seventy years! More pertinent, however, was the fact that Kohl possessed a fine two-wheel trap and horse: the same trap and horse that had not only transported Holmes to the town of Hohenschwangau, but also his brother Mycroft just a few days before him.

Despite the lateness of the hour, Kohl was more than happy to repeat that journey with me on board, provided the fare matched those of his earlier passengers. I did not hesitate for an instant in making this payment and before too long we began the three-mile journey to Hohenschwangau, a town that I prayed would prove to be my final port of call.

We crossed the River Lech over the Fussener Strassen and I soon discovered that, between that bridge and our intended destination, lay nothing but dark, pine-lined dirt tracks. In that shadowy and claustrophobic silence, the sound of the horse's hooves upon the gravel achieved a stark, repetitive resonance that filled the air. The elderly beast and its driver had probably made this journey a hundred times or more, and therefore knew the location of every stone and divot, thus rendering my journey a surprisingly smooth and comfortable one.

Needless to say, our slow progress created the illusion that the distance between Fussen and Hohenschwangau was considerably further than its supposed three miles. I filled and lit my pipe, and bemoaned the fact that the surrounding natural wonders were slowly becoming obscured by the deepening gloom.

Suddenly a brisk breeze swept down from those dizzying peaks and dramatically swept the clouds away from the blue, three-quarter moon. The terrain was now doused in its shimmering light, and the imperious trees became all the more imposing.

Finally, as we rounded a long, steep bend, I saw it! There, in the distance, reared the magnificent towers and romantic parapets of the castle of Neuschwanstein, its ornate lines surrounded by the searing peaks that it emulated so well.

CHAPTER FOUR

REUNIONS

There was something absurdly surreal about the elaborate Romanesque architecture of the place and it was obvious at first glance that its occupant valued its seclusion and inaccessibility far more than its discretion and anonymity.

My reflections were interrupted by another sharp bend in the road and the return of that curtain of cloud. We did not see the castle again before we finally arrived on the outskirts of Hohenschwangau. As I grabbed my bag from the back of the cart and paid my driver his fare, I voiced my misgivings of the fact that he was about to make that long, dark return journey on his own.

Peter Kohl the younger merely emitted a high-pitched and toothless cackle while he lifted up a wooden flap that was fitted under his seat. I was assured of his safety by the sight of an enormous blunderbuss that nestled ominously within its box. I slapped the horse's neck appreciatively and watched for a few moments while the two of them sank once more into the shadows.

With a light and determined step I made my way towards the lake of Alpseebad, around which the majority of the town was set. However, even now, at the very apex of my journey, I soon came to realise that my long search was not yet over.

The town boasted several suitable hostelries and, consequently, it was well past nightfall by the time that I finally staggered up the steps of the last of these, the Gasthaus Muller. My relief, upon discovering that the place still held one last vacancy, almost superseded my despondency when my description of the Holmes brothers was met by nothing more positive than a blank expression and an exaggerated shrug of the shoulders.

With an exhausted resignation, I handed my bag to a young pageboy, that he might lead me to my room. Could my calculations and planning have been so wrong? Were Holmes's designs to exclude me from this adventure going to prove themselves to be so complete and successful?

Dejected, I slowly followed the page up the stairs until I was stopped in my tracks by a familiar smell. Surely that was the pungent aroma of Holmes's favourite old shag tobacco wafting towards me from the e saloon! I handed my key to the page and then strode purposefully towards the source of that overwhelming odour.

'Ah, Watson! Your arrival is several hours later than I would have expected!' From behind the wings of a large fireside chair, a strident voice rang out — one that I had so often feared I would never hear again.

My sense of relief was such that I approached the chair in a breathless silence. Sure enough, there was my friend Sherlock Holmes smiling broadly through a thick plume of smoke, sitting opposite his brother Mycroft, who was similarly engaged with a large cigar. The brothers were clearly amused at my nonplussed reaction to my discovery, and they had both been cradling a warming glass of cognac.

'Welcome, Dr Watson, you have done well, sir!' Mycroft boomed, while Holmes moved another chair across, to create a small and discreet circle.

Once I had been furnished with a cognac of my own, the Holmes's demanded to know the thought processes and the chain of events that had led to my arrival at the Gasthaus Muller on that very night. This, of course, I was more than happy to do, and once I had concluded my long narrative they both offered me their congratulations.

'This is all very well,' I protested. 'However, the lengths that you have gone to in order to distract me from my path, had led me to the conclusion that you did not wish me to contribute to this quest at all! Nevertheless, the only surprise that you have expressed at my appearance was the lateness of my arrival, almost as if my success had always been a foregone conclusion. I confess that I do not understand.'

'Oh Watson, of course your presence here was desirable, otherwise I would not have sent you the message from Sigurdsson in the first place, nor would I have furnished you with any clues whatsoever.'

Holmes pulled his chair closer to mine and his countenance altered disturbingly. When he next spoke, his voice had dropped to a whisper. Clearly the lateness of the hour, together with the warmth of the fire and the cognac, had taken their toll on Holmes's elder brother, for his cigar was now hanging limply from his lower lip and his eyes were fighting a losing battle at remaining open.

'You must understand, Watson, that the reach and scope of our enemies is far broader and deeper than anything that even I could have imagined. The brief sketch that Mycroft has supplied me with, since my arrival, has been enough to convince me that my caution, before leaving Baker Street, had been totally justified.

'Had my course of action been more obvious to you, the chances were that it would be so to our enemies as well. I could not take the risk that they might find their way to Mycroft before I could reach him. Therefore, I decided to leave you a meagre and a more subtle scattering of breadcrumbs, knowing full well that my Watson would be more than capable of picking up my trail. Your very presence here absolutely vindicates my faith in you and your potential value to our little enterprise.' Holmes smiled proudly, but

I wondered at his flippant description of the task that lay ahead of us.

'Thank you, Holmes. Now I understand.'

'Nevertheless,' he continued, 'before we can put our plans into motion, my brother here has much to explain to you. As I have told you, he has only briefly outlined the magnitude and the significance of the knowledge that he has accumulated. As you can see, however, now would not seem to be the most appropriate time for such revelations.' Holmes gently shook Mycroft by the shoulder and then suggested that we all make our way upstairs, for what could prove to be our last comfortable night's sleep for quite some time.

As might be imagined, these were sentiments with which I wholeheartedly concurred.

CHAPTER FIVE

ENCOUNTERS

As it transpired, my night's sleep had proved to be everything that I had hoped for and had undoubtedly required. So much so, in fact, that by the time that I eventually managed to rouse myself and descend the stairs, Sherlock Holmes and his brother were already engaged with their breakfast.

I immediately followed suit and noticed that Mycroft was devouring his plateful of eggs, bread and Bratwurst with a gusto that had been similar to my own. All the while, Holmes smiled with amusement at the sight of our gastronomic indulgence as he extinguished his cigarette in his partially filled cup of coffee.

'Gentlemen, I suggest that we retire to a more discreet location before Mycroft begins to outline the results of his research and his strategy for the coming days. That is, once you have both concluded your gluttonous ritual, of course.'

Holmes pushed back his chair and rose, before Mycroft and I even had the chance to complete our last mouthfuls. Obviously, we had both followed suit immediately, and Holmes then led us to a small, secluded terrace at the rear of the building.

Once Holmes was satisfied that we should not be overheard, and as soon as we had all filled and lit our pipes, Mycroft sank back into his chair and clasped his hands together, across his corpulent waistline.

'Dr Watson, I am happy to report that your hypothesis that it was I who had arranged for the early release of the notorious Roger Ashley was a correct one. However, I am equally certain that my motives for doing so were entirely different to the ones that you and my brother might have surmised. I can assure you that they had nothing to do with the recovery of the stolen mandolin, despite its apparent importance and intrinsic value. As a matter of fact, I would say that its recovery is nothing more than a point of mere trivia. Furthermore, my objectives had nothing to do with my allaying the threat to my brother's life, posed by Gruner's psychotic thirst for revenge. I, too, had realised that the succession of crimes with which Sherlock had been confronted in London had been designed to lure him towards an untimely demise here in Bavaria.

'My agents' investigations had led me to the conclusion that there were yet more urgent matters that required my personal attention. A number of prearranged encounters that they had with various members of Gruner's staff, seemed to indicate that Gruner was nothing less than the central power behind the Austrian cell of the Bavarian Brotherhood!

'From that you might infer that his choice of Neuschwanstein Castle was not merely based upon its total isolation and impregnability. More pertinent, perhaps, is the fact that it lies no further than three miles from the Austro/ Bavarian border.

'My brother may have been surprised that I could be motivated enough to extricate myself from my regular habits and routines in such a dynamic fashion, and the very idea of my expending so much time and energy in making this journey would have seemed ludicrous in the extreme. However, I can assure you, Dr Watson, that I should never have even considered making such sacrifices had my agents not convinced me of the urgency and potentially dire consequence of the matter.'

Mycroft paused for a moment while he put a match to his pipe, and I glanced across to observe the effect that his revelations were having upon my friend. I was rather surprised to note that Holmes was reclining comfortably in his chair, his eyes tightly shut, with barely an indication upon his inscrutable face that Mycroft's words had even resonated with him.

'Watson, you really should not confuse relaxed indifference with the deepest of concentration,' said he, as if conscious of my tacit surprise.

'Well upon my word, Holmes,' I exclaimed, 'you really must have translucent eyelids!'

Holmes's eyes flashed open momentarily and he allowed himself the briefest of smiles.

'I just know, my Watson,' he stated quietly as he closed his eyes once more.

Mycroft appeared to have been oblivious to this brief exchange and he continued in a similar vein as he had before.

'You see, Dr Watson, my brother and I agree upon one thing. If ever a man was deserving of the gallows, then that man would certainly be Herr Gruner. I happen to know as fact that the rumours surrounding the untimely death of his wife and an observant young goat herder were anything but hearsay. However, my privileged insights into Gruner's other intrigues require that he be allowed his liberty for just a short while longer.

'Unfortunately, my brother is still under the rather naive impression that he has been handed the mantle of being a custodian of justice. Consequently, the notion that a man such as Gruner be allowed to escape his fate is abhorrent to him.

'To allay your fears, however, I can assure you both that once I have extracted the information that I require of him, Gruner will surely face the dire consequences of his actions. We must act quickly though, for once his confederates are made aware of his fall, their plans will change within a heartbeat.'

Upon hearing Mycroft's use of the word 'naive', I heard my friend emit a brief suppressed laugh, and his eyes sprang back open once he sensed that Mycroft had reached the end of his declaration.

'I believe that the word you were searching for was "ideological" rather than naive. In that, brother, we are not so dissimilar. However, whereas my primary objective is the preservation of justice for, and the welfare of, unfortunate individuals, your concerns encompass an entire nation!'

'Well said, Sherlock; as you say, we are indeed not so different after all.' Mycroft suddenly got to his feet and clapped his hands together resoundingly, as if to galvanise us into immediate action.

'Gentlemen, I am afraid that I have to ask you both to sacrifice your comfortable rooms upstairs for a rather more rudimentary form of accommodation. Once we have arrived there and taken possession, I am certain that my explanation for having to make such a concession will become clearer to you.'

With an exuberance that caught Holmes and I off our guard, Mycroft ushered us both back up to our rooms, and he would not relent with his encouragement until we were all downstairs at the front desk with our bags packed and ready for an immediate departure.

To our surprise, we were greeted at the front door by the sight of Peter Kohl the younger aboard his cart and with his trusty steed stomping its front hooves with impatience.

'Guten Morgen, Herr Mannlich!' Kohl greeted us cheerily while doffing his feathered hat. Despite his friendly reception, he made no effort at assisting us with our bags and once Mycroft had appropriated the seat next to Kohl, Holmes and I knew at once that we would be sharing the back of the cart with the bags.

Therefore, it was in this most uncomfortable of fashion that we set off upon our journey to Mycroft's mysterious location.

CHAPTER SIX

A RENDEZVOUS AT THE LODGE

As we slowly took our leave of Hohenschwangau, I looked back over my shoulder towards the Gasthaus Muller with a mixture of regret and trepidation, for we were certainly embarking upon a journey into the unknown.

In the distance we could see the Marienbrucke, an elegant yet unnervingly narrow suspension bridge that had been named after Queen Marie, the mother of the castle's builder, King Ludwig II. Although the bridge afforded a perfect view of the castle, the seditious nature of our enterprise required a rather more guarded and obscure approach.

A moment later both the castle and the bridge disappeared from our view as we slowly became engulfed by the dense, all-consuming forest.

It was certainly evident that Mycroft's objectives had been meticulously planned, because neither our driver nor his horse had hesitated for a second as they navigated their path through the labyrinth of protruding roots and the trunks of fallen giants that seemed to have been designed to inhibit our progress. Despite the camouflage afforded by those ancient trees, I knew that each step was bringing us ever closer to

Neuschwanstein, and my heart quickened at the thought of the adventures that might lie ahead.

We continued in this fashion for what seemed to have been an interminable length of time, until we eventually arrived within a flat, yet overgrowing clearing. In its centre was set a small, stout, oak-built hunting lodge that showed every sign of many years of neglect. Despite its state of disrepair, the lodge still boasted an ornate coat of arms, which adorned the arch above its front door. Undoubtedly this building had once served as the royal hunting lodge of King Ludwig II.

The sparse furnishings within showed that Ludwig had spent as little time here as he had within his cherished castle. However, Mycroft had prepared well for a short stay, and I was pleased to note that the lodge had been adequately supplied with food and fire fuel.

Once we had unloaded our belongings, Kohl took his leave of us once more, and I was left wondering as to our subsequent means of transport. Mycroft led us to the back of the lodge, where we found three magnificent bays, well fed and watered, and tethered to a post. Mycroft was not oblivious to my dubious appraisal of his transportation plans.

'You should not be so surprised, Dr Watson,' said he, 'for I was riding from a very early age and my animal is far sturdier than yours!'

Holmes clapped his hands gleefully.

'You have done well, brother Mycroft! The location of our base could not have been better chosen. We are invisible to any curious observer within the castle, but close enough to be able to make our final assault on foot. However, you have been rather less than frugal with the details of what you expect us to discover within those castle walls, and your intentions, from this point onwards, are, as yet, a blank page.'

'Gentlemen,' Mycroft announced with a smile, 'we have a long night ahead of us, but first of all I think we should make use of the contents of my bag.'

Whereupon he proceeded to set out upon the table the ingredients for a more than adequate cold supper. There was a selection of various local meats, chunks of delicious rough bread, and a bottle of Riesling. He had even remembered some wooden plates and goblets to complete this humble feast, and to my surprise, Holmes indulged in its destruction with gusto.

It was only once the last mouthful had been digested and we had lit our cigars by the fire that Mycroft decided to outline his plans to us.

'My expectations of what you shall discover within Gruner's castle are somewhat vaguer than you might have expected. However, my agents have informed me that in recent weeks Gruner has been receiving more guests than at any time previously. The nature of these clandestine meetings is unknown to us at this time, but they are undoubtedly of the greatest moment.'

'How are you able to know this?' Holmes asked, leaning forward in his chair.

'My people have observed a succession of prominent businessmen and politicians arrive at the most unsociable of hours, each one clutching attaché cases and then being ushered into Gruner's private study, wherein hushed and surreptitious meetings have taken place. These bags have appeared to be somewhat thinner upon the departure of these illustrious guests, leading us to the conclusion that certain papers have been secured within the desk of Gruner's study.'

'Your evaluation seems to be sound,' Holmes confirmed.

'We think so. You should also be glad to know that your ability to gain access to this desk will not be as difficult as you might imagine. I happen to know that there are no guests present at the moment and Gruner's only companions are Roger Ashley, of such ill repute, three permanent guards, and only two other members of staff, who just happen to be of my acquaintance.' Mycroft smiled with an obvious air of self-satisfaction.

'This is all very well,' I protested, 'but you have made no mention of how we are to gain access to this fortress, or of your plans subsequent to us ransacking Gruner's desk.'

'I have held discussions with the local police force, informing them of Gruner's former crimes, although precious little else, I might add. Obviously, since these crimes were perpetrated within their jurisdiction, they are more than enthusiastic in providing their cooperation.

'On the night after next, a small force of mounted officers will await your signal from within the outer fringes of the tree line. This signal will tell them that Gruner is ready to be taken, but nothing other than that. They understand that their primary objective is to ensure that Gruner should not escape. Aside from that,' Mycroft concluded emphatically, 'I can assure you that I have no intention of allowing them access to any other information.'

'It would seem that you have as little faith in the abilities of the local constabulary as I have in their London-based counterparts,' Holmes jovially observed.

Mycroft's confirmation was a broad smile and a nod of his head, after which he suggested that we all retire for the night.

'Your means of access to the castle will become apparent to you tomorrow evening,' Mycroft promised enigmatically in response to our questioning glances. He then laid down some blankets upon the floor. Rather sensibly, as it transpired, Mycroft remained in his chair throughout the night.

When Holmes and I stirred the following morning, there was neither a muscle nor a joint which did not ache excruciatingly. Holmes suggested and demonstrated a number of stretching exercises, which proved to be surprisingly effective, and by the time Mycroft had boiled up some water on the fire for our coffee, all traces of that uncomfortable night had dissipated.

We spent most of that day on long walks and quiet reflection, and once the remains of the previous night's supper had been cleared away, Mycroft presented us with a large canvas bag, in which we would remove Gruner's documents, and a small lantern that would be our means of sending our signal to the mounted police.

Holmes was about to raise the subject of our assault upon the castle once more, when we were surprised by a sharp knock upon the lodge door.

'Come in! Come in!' Mycroft boomed and an instant later his invitation was accepted.

The appearance of the two individuals, who now stood before us in the doorway, could not have been more disparate. The first to move forward and consequently to close the door behind them was a wizened and elderly servant who went by the name of Gabriel.

Clearly Gabriel had been amused by the looks of disappointment upon the faces of both Holmes and I. Therefore, presumably as a means of proving his worth, he raised his height by several inches simply by straightening his back and, with an open smile, he extended a strong hand to each of us, which we readily accepted.

His companion was a most impressive individual indeed. Ara Vukovic was strikingly tall and attractive, and dressed from head to toe in black. She was doubtless aware of my admiration, for she distracted herself by incessantly tossing her luxuriant mane of red hair back and forth. I was surprised to note that about her waist hung a wide, brown leather belt, which housed both a sabre and a substantial looking revolver.

Mycroft clapped his hands resoundingly while he introduced the four of us.

'These two will prove to be your means of gaining access both to the castle and the desk of Herr Gruner!' Mycroft exclaimed, and he went on to outline the years of meticulous planning that had gone into the success of this mission.

'Both Miss Vukovic and young Gabriel here have slowly ingratiated their way into Gruner's household. Tomorrow night it will be Gabriel's task to unbolt and leave open a small, but otherwise impassable, tradesmen's entrance, which is set into the basement of the main keep. Once you have passed through, he will hold this door with his life until such time as your position inside is secure.

'As you have both doubtless observed, Miss Vukovic's talents are of an entirely different, and deadlier, nature. Long before her involvement here, she has served my department well as a most relentless and accomplished assassin! I can assure you both that she is as skilled with the revolver as she is with the sabre.

'Once you have entered the castle, she will guide you from the basement to Gruner's study and then ensure that you have as much time inside as she can buy. I should warn you, however, that this may not be as long as you would like. The guards might be few, but they are vigilant. Only once you have gleaned Gruner's papers might the signal to the police be sent.

'Without a doubt the dangers and the potential pitfalls are obvious, but you should be under no illusions, the stakes are the highest that you have ever played for and your success could save millions of lives!'

Mycroft's words sent a chill of excitement and, I must admit, fear running down my spine. I looked across to my friend for reassurance, but to my surprise he appeared to be more interested in Miss Vukovic than in Mycroft's dire warnings. Throughout our association, Holmes had only ever expressed admiration for one other woman, but even Irene Adler had failed to captivate Holmes in any manner other than a professional one. Miss Vukovic had left him nonplussed and his eyes even followed her when Mycroft warned our guests that they might soon be missed at the castle and then unceremoniously bundled them out of the lodge.

Mycroft's exertions had clearly exhausted him and once he had fallen asleep in his chair by the fire, I suggested that Holmes and I take our last pipes outside, that I might raise the subject of Miss Vukovic with him, while out of earshot of his brother.

We strolled around the perimeter of the lodge in silence for a while and the icy stillness of the night exaggerated and amplified the sound of our boots crunching into the brittle soil.

'Miss Vukovic is certainly a most impressive young woman, wouldn't you say?' I asked mischievously.

'Whatever do you mean?' Holmes responded with a feigned indifference.

'Oh, come along, Holmes, you know precisely what I am talking about. For heaven's sake, your eyes did not leave her once, even up to the very moment that she left the room. I would even be so bold as to say that you barely seemed to acknowledge or digest a single word of your brother's vital arrangements.'

'My dear Watson, if you are referring to the woman's bearing and deportment, then I grant you that there was certainly much to commend her. However, if, as I strongly suspect, you were alluding also to her comeliness, then I must remind you that it has long been a maxim of mine to ignore any aspect of a case that might divert me from its logical and satisfactory conclusion. Watson, I need not remind you that we are about to enter the lair of a most dangerous and formidable foe. Therefore, if we are to commend our success and even survival into the hands of any individual, even one with such obvious credentials and recommendations, it is only logical that I try to ascertain her capabilities and nature with but a few moments of careful study and observation.' Holmes concluded his explanation with an air of self-satisfaction that I found to be irksome in the extreme.

'Well, of course that would be your way of rationalising your conduct. However, you cannot convince me, even for an instant, that you learned enough to assure you of her value to our expedition or to justify your most singular behaviour.'

'Watson, you seem to forget that we are not all as susceptible to the allures of the fairer sex as you are. I merely see Miss Vukovic as another tool to aid us in our quest and, I would suggest, of no greater value to us than her partner, Gabriel.

'I would now strongly recommend that we take to our blankets without further delay. The night turns colder still and the next twenty-four hours or so will demand much of our energy and resolve.'

Without a moment's hesitation, I dutifully followed Holmes back into the lodge, although I knew that any thoughts of slumber would likely be negated by my constantly reverberating mind.

CHAPTER SEVEN

A MOONLIT ASSAULT

That night I slept a fitful and fretful sleep and it was easy for me to understand the reason why.

My mind had been full of castles and assassins, bemused by international conspiracies and with Baron Gruner and the part that he had to play in all of this. Above all, however, it had been the thrill of the unknown dangers that might be lurking within those soaring walls and towers that had kept my mind so active.

Mycroft had outlined his plans in a clear and precise manner, as if in his mind the outcome had always been a foregone conclusion. I, however, had also been fully aware of the potential pitfalls that might have presented themselves and I had been equally concerned by the distracted manner in which Holmes had received his brother's strategic plans.

My friend had appeared so obsessed by the statuesque assassin who had presented herself at the lodge, that I even doubted whether Holmes had been aware of the role that Mycroft had assigned to Miss Vukovic, or of any other part of his stratagem, for that matter.

My sleepless state had not been helped either by the uncomfortable floor, nor the inadequate blankets with which Mycroft had presented us. Of course, the fire had expired long before we had retired and so I finally I abandoned my efforts and slipped quietly outside for a cigarette and an opportunity to bathe in the glow of the vibrant moon.

However, this reverie of mine was not to last long, for the intense cold soon forced me back inside to the sanctuary of my threadbare blanket. Upon waking the following morning, I was disappointed to note that Mycroft's rations had not extended to a breakfast, save for a cup or coarse black coffee. Obviously, this abstinence did not present Sherlock Holmes with any great difficulties. After all, this form of deprivation had so often been self-imposed by my friend as a means of preserving his energy when engaged upon a difficult case. Consequently, he had been positively chipper when he finally joined us around the fire.

'Well, I must say, brother Mycroft, that you have positively excelled yourself with the meticulous and detailed nature of your planning. Contrary to the presumptions of Dr Watson here, I managed to absorb every word, and I believe that you have managed to allow for every contingency, save for those instinctive reactions that are so often prevalent in a man in jeopardy.'

'Do you not approve of my choice of accomplices?' Mycroft asked, clearly confused by his brother's reservations.

'On the contrary, Miss Vukovic appears to be a most assured and accomplished young woman. However, before we embark upon such a hazardous mission, I would like to know the precise nature of the documents that we are risking so much in obtaining.'

Mycroft removed his monocle and eyed his brother quizzically from beneath a raised and bushy eyebrow.

'I am afraid that in that respect I cannot further enlighten you. We have been reliably informed that the papers are of the greatest importance and that they contain the precise nature of the Brotherhood's far-reaching plans. Other than that, I can only assure you that there is far more gravitas attached to this problem than the petty little cases with which you have been presented with in London.'

Holmes slapped the arm of his chair angrily and jumped to his feet.

'That simply is not good enough, Mycroft!' he exclaimed. 'I cannot in all good conscience allow Dr Watson to place himself in such peril for the sake of a few papers whose contents might yet prove to be of little consequence.'

I was most surprised and, I must admit, rather gratified to hear Holmes expressing his concerns for my welfare in such a manner.

'If you regard the very continuance of our society and way of life to be of little consequence,' boomed Mycroft, 'then by all means abandon this enterprise now and hurry back to the safety and comfort of your rooms in Baker Street!'

Holmes smiled at his brother's unusual display of passion, and without another word we all went about our final preparations.

The day had passed slowly indeed and I had lost count of the number of times that I had cleaned and reloaded my revolver. Mycroft had ensured that his brother had been similarly armed, but Holmes seemed to put more faith in his favoured, weight-loaded cane.

As the appointed time finally approached, the misgivings that I had been harbouring for so long finally gave way to those of relief and elation, so tedious had been the last few hours. Mycroft bade us farewell from the lodge door, although Holmes refused to stride out until he had heard its huge bolt being thrown by his brother.

The density of the forest allowed us a certain freedom of movement as we began our approach. However, as we drew closer to the castle, the trees began to thin out and the brilliant three-quarter moon, which shimmered majestically above the icy landscape, presented us with a double-edged sword. It certainly provided us with the means of negotiating the testing landscape safely, but we were also aware of the fact that it could highlight us to any curious eyes that might have been peering down from the battlements of Neuschwanstein Castle. We slowed our progress considerably, while at the same time reducing our stature by assuming a most painful crouching position throughout the remainder of our journey.

Holmes and I had been somewhat perturbed to note that the small troop of mounted police had assumed a position far closer to the castle than that which had been described to us by Mycroft. Nevertheless, they had managed to maintain their position in a motionless silence and Holmes and I pushed on determinedly towards the thick wooden door that was set into the base of the wall and concealed behind the castle's imposing entrance. I was certain that, had it not been for Mycroft's precise directions, we would have struggled to have found it at all, so discreetly had it been set.

Our discreet approach had been further aided by a voluminous mist that had unexpectedly descended from the surrounding mountain peaks. This shroud had fallen so quickly that the lofty spires appeared to have become suddenly disembodied from their supporting walls and, at first glance, one would have supposed that they were actually floating in the night sky.

We arrived at the door certain in the knowledge that we had remained undetected throughout. Certainly, any would-be observer from above would have needed to possess a most dextrous neck in order to spy upon us now. Holmes glanced down at his timepiece, and his gesture to me indicated that we had arrived ahead of schedule.

We lit and smoked our cigarettes in absolute silence, but the ensuing delay produced an unbearable strain upon my nerves. I gazed at Holmes in admiration, for he had accepted this protracted delay with an implausible, stoic resolve. Holmes brought out his watch once more and on this occasion he tapped its glass to draw my attention to the time.

I stepped forward and proceeded to rap upon the door in a prearranged sequence. The lack of an immediate response to this signal convinced me that something untoward had overtaken our elderly ally, and that our game had been up before it had barely begun. Nevertheless, Holmes remained resolute and he restrained me from repeating the cipher with a surprisingly firm grip upon my forearm.

Finally, with a silence that belied its age, a bolt was slowly pulled back and the otherwise impenetrable door gradually opened. Gabriel had been barely able to create a gap large enough through which Holmes and I could comfortably pass, such had been the weight of this imposing barrier. Nevertheless, we squeezed through it in an instant and then assisted the old man in re-closing the door.

Once the bolt had been replaced, Gabriel led us along a dark and seldom used corridor towards a large spiral staircase that would lead us to the vigilant Miss Vukovic. Despite our having been forewarned of the paucity of Gruner's companions, the desolate stillness that permeated those vast and endless halls still took me by surprise. Therefore, Gabriel's earnest appeal for silence could not have been more unnecessary, for I had become convinced that even a fallen feather would have set off an echo within those stony halls and towers.

Once we had negotiated our way to the base of the stairs without incident, Gabriel assured us in a barely audible tone that both of Gruner's uniformed guards were patrolling the castle's outer perimeter. His knowledge of their schedule convinced him that we had more than enough time in which to gain access to Gruner's private study.

Gabriel became quite agitated once he had realised the time and he hurried off to the far tower, where he would shortly be serving drinks to Gruner and Roger Ashley. Before scurrying away, Gabriel waved us towards the staircase, indicating that we should climb them without delay. Neither Holmes nor I needed to be told twice and we bounded up the stairs three at a time until we breathlessly arrived at the feet of Miss Vukovic.

With neither a word nor sign of greeting she led us towards a pair of impressive oak doors, which boasted the same coat of arms that we had observed above the entrance to the hunting lodge. Once again I noticed Holmes steal an admiring glance at the young assassin, although I was certain that it was only born of his admiration for her bravery.

She took up a position outside the room while he tinkered feverishly with the lock, using a small instrument that he always carried within his infamous toolkit. The Amazonian sentinel stood to attention, firmly planting both hands upon her hips, the left above her holster and the right upon the hilt of her sword. To any potential opponent, there would have been very little doubt as to her resolve and intent.

Evidently the lock's mechanism was rather complex, for several agonising minutes had passed before Holmes eventually found success. He ushered me through the door with a sharp tug on my sleeve and instructed me to guard the entrance with an impatient wave of his hand.

Holmes soon discovered that only one of the desk's drawers was actually locked and of course it was there that he concentrated his search. Another instrument from his kit was brought into use and a moment later he began to fill Mycroft's satchel with as many reams of papers as he could gather. As I stood vigil, I could not help but wonder at the magnificent, Romanesque architecture with which the place was so plentifully and spectacularly endowed. The castle's previous tenant had undoubtedly been a man with a grandiose vision and no sense of modesty whatsoever.

My observations and reflections were soon brought to an abrupt halt by the sounds of a commotion echoing along the vast corridor outside. These sounds were highlighted by a surprisingly high-pitched shriek of warning from Miss Vukovic, and I lost no time in investigating its cause.

Leaving Holmes to his task, I pulled out my revolver and slammed the door shut behind me as I hurried from the room. Gruner's guards had raised the alarm, and they were also aware of Gabriel's treachery. They were speeding towards us, guns at the ready, leaving behind them the prostrate body of our elderly ally, whose head was bleeding profusely from a vicious blow to his skull!

We halted the progress of the guards with a series of rapid volleys from our guns. The guards took shelter behind the stone pillars that lined each passageway, but they didn't venture beyond them until they saw Gruner and Roger Ashley running towards us from the opposite direction. We were trapped!

To my horror, it was at this very moment that Holmes emerged from the study, unaware of the imminent danger into which he was entering. At the sight of Holmes, Gruner emitted a horrific cry, no doubt realising Holmes's intent. That callous and devious man appeared all the more sinister behind his black silk mask, but he was forced to retreat by my careful aim.

Ashley, however, was not so easily put off and he lunged at Holmes with his sabre raised. In a single flowing movement, Miss Vukovic unsheathed her own weapon and tossed it to Holmes, who had grasped it at the very moment of Ashley's attempted strike.

The three of us were fighting on two fronts, but to further add to the confusion and with total disregard for Mycroft's instructions, the police had broken ranks at the sound of the gunfire and were attempting to force an access. In the absence of Gabriel, this proved to be no easy task, and our enemies were edging ever closer towards us.

After a breathless exchange with Ashley, Holmes's attention was drawn to the sight of Gruner scurrying away down the corridor in the opposite direction.

'Quickly, Watson,' he called to me. 'In breaking ranks the police have allowed Gruner the opportunity of escape!'

I turned towards Gruner's direction, but the gunfire of his guards prevented me from running after him. He was in the company of a tall, blonde-haired woman, who we subsequently discovered to be his daughter, and even she carried a gun, which she used against me.

The situation had been an impossible one and had it not been for the timely intervention of the police, I am certain that our cause would have been lost. A deafening volley of gunfire put paid to Gruner's guards, but the police were unable to halt the flight of Gruner and his daughter, who had disappeared down a hidden stairway.

However, my attention had been drawn to the plight of my friend. Despite his undoubted skill with a blade, Holmes had been constantly on the retreat from the very beginning of their confrontation. His momentum had allowed Ashley the opportunity to test Holmes with a series of swings and thrusts that Holmes struggled to parry.

The police were unable to intervene with their revolvers due to the close proximity in which Holmes and Ashley were fighting. Even a slight deviation of our aim would undoubtedly have resulted in a fatal outcome for my friend. So we looked on helplessly as the battle moved ever closer to a narrow stairway that led to the highest of the castle's turrets.

Half of the force followed in Gruner's wake, although they were finally stopped in their tracks by the sound of a carriage and a team of four clattering down the drive and away from the castle. Unless Holmes had procured papers of significant value, all of our efforts would now prove to have been futile. They examined the sad, still form of the brave Gabriel, but their concern and attention were all too obviously in vain.

I left the police to the business of questioning Miss Vukovic and examining the remains of Gruner's guards, and began to edge tentatively towards the stairway that Holmes and Ashley had begun to slowly ascend. Any thoughts that I might have had of letting off a shot were precluded by the constrictive space in which the two antagonists were fighting.

Holmes was being forced to retreat up the stairs, but the words that they had been exchanging, with a fervour similar to that employed in their cuts and thrusts, had been drowned out by the howling mountain winds that were swept down the stairs towards me. Nevertheless, from the tones of his raised voice, I could tell that Ashley was attempting to goad and provoke my friend into a rash and inappropriate action. Then I lost sight of them.

I slowly and cautiously crept up the stairs behind them, in the hope that my revolver might yet be brought into play. As I neared the top of the tower I was shaken by the chill of the air and the ferocity of the wind, but my intent to help Holmes overrode any of my misgivings or discomfort.

The scene that greeted me, as I finally reached the summit, took my breath away. Holmes had lost his hat and his hair flew into his face. Ashley's eyes flashed wildly as he pressed home his advantage and each stroke of his sword forced Holmes ever backwards. The wind had whipped the clouds up into a frenzied dance and each time that they crossed the moon, the protagonists were engulfed in a temporary darkness. Obviously, this banished any thoughts that I might have had of letting off a volley and I could only watch helplessly as this duel moved inexorably towards its climax. However, its conclusion was not as obvious as I had once feared. Of the two men, Ashley was now breathing the hardest and his provocative banter had been silenced by Holmes's steely resolve.

Ashley's strokes were becoming wild and impulsive, while Holmes was holding his form. Holmes began to repel Ashley's attacks with a calm confidence and when another flash of Ashley's blade missed its mark, Holmes thrust forward and the point of his sword found its target with deep and bloody penetration.

Ashley was as surprised as he had been dismayed, and his sabre clattered to the floor with a dull empty echo. He clutched at his heart with both hands and while Holmes and I looked on helplessly, Gruner's accomplice tipped over the turret's edge with a bloodcurdling cry that almost drowned out the howls of the mountain storm.

Holmes and I gazed down into the icy abyss into which Roger Ashley had been consumed and we knew that its hidden depths would forever be his final resting place. To my surprise, however, Holmes had been more concerned by the sight of Gruner's carriage careering away from the castle, than with the awful consequences of his actions.

'You see, Watson, once again the ineptitude of the regular force may have jeopardised the success of our quest. Gruner will undoubtedly do everything in his power to reclaim his papers and seek to exact an awful revenge!'

Suddenly his grip on my left shoulder caused me to cry out in pain.

'Mycroft!' he cried. 'We must go to Mycroft!' There was genuine terror in his voice as he forced me to follow him back down the stairs.

CHAPTER EIGHT

FLIGHT

Holmes and I raced recklessly down the stairs and did not even pause to observe or acknowledge the considerable damage caused to the tradesman's door by the destructive entrance made by the police.

Outside, we were confronted by the sight of the police horses that had been tethered loosely to a nearby tree stump. Holmes and I exchanged furtive glances of excitement and without a moment's hesitation we grabbed the bridles of the two most likely candidates and segregated them from the others.

We calmed the beasts to silence by gently stroking their forelocks and once we were certain that we had not been observed, we climbed aboard our chosen mounts and rode slowly away without harbouring even a moment's guilt.

Once we had reached the security of the forest, we broke out of a canter and induced a slow gallop from our mounts. We wound our way through the pines and thickets with care, conscious of the potential need for urgency. Finally, when Holmes's anxiety had reached a crescendo, we neared the edge of the clearing, where we could see the outline of the hunting lodge in the distance.

When we were within a hundred yards of the place, we decided to dismount and lead the horses on foot, for fear of disturbing any would-be intruder with the sound of our approach. We tethered the reins to a small handrail and crept carefully towards an undraped window.

Holmes peered tentatively through the misty glass and then beckoned for me to join him with a small smile. Our worst fears had been unfounded, for there was Mycroft Holmes, seated in front of a dying fire with his corpulent chin folded comfortably into his chest, fast asleep and mercifully unharmed.

We awoke him with a simultaneous sharp rap upon the window and a resounding knock upon the lodge door. Even then it was some time before Mycroft managed to raise himself to let us in.

'My dear fellow,' Mycroft boomed as he led us towards the fire, 'although I must confess to some surprise, I also find it entirely gratifying to note your concern for your brother's well-being.'

'Whatever do you mean?' asked Holmes, although his attempt at feigning ignorance of his brother's meaning was far from being a successful one.

'Oh, come along Sherlock; please do not imply that I am incapable of recognising extreme anxiety upon a man's face when I see it. Equally, when I observe two police horses tethered close by, I cannot fail to draw the conclusion that you had decided that the police force's pursuit of Baron Gruner was of a lower priority than you galloping here to come to my rescue!' Mycroft smiled at his brother's discomfort.

'You actually thought it more probable that Gruner would go out of his way to harass an old man, as opposed to executing his own successful flight?' Mycroft asked incredulously.

'I thought it not unlikely,' admitted Holmes reluctantly.

'I would regard such an option as being extremely unlikely!' Mycroft exclaimed. 'Even had Gruner known of the lodge's existence and location, which he did not, I might add, he would have realised that you had not the time to reach the lodge with the papers, before his arrival. Believe me when I tell you that the recovery of the contents of his desk is his overriding priority, for without those his life is not worth a moment's purchase.'

Mycroft clapped his hands together resoundingly and invited us to sit down and help ourselves to the contents of his cigar case.

'Notwithstanding my concerns over your illogical and, may I say, emotional chain of thought, Sherlock, I am extremely grateful for the exertions you went through on my behalf,' Mycroft confessed. Holmes merely cleared his throat and put an ember from the fire to his cigar with a set of log tongs.

'I trust that you have also given consideration to the probability that Gruner will now be even more hell-bent on revenge?' Holmes enquired. 'My previous experience of the man strongly suggests such a motivation.'

'Naturally I have,' Mycroft confirmed, 'but he will only do so on his own terms. You seem to forget that years of extensive research and planning have gone into tonight's little exercise, and I can assure you that my knowledge of Herr Gruner is every bit as incisive as yours. When I tell you that the recovery of the papers is his primary motivation, you may take it as the absolute truth.'

As I sat there observing the two brothers engaging in this analysis, I realised that in many respects they were not so dissimilar after all. The disparities in their appearance were more than obvious, even to an untrained eye. Although of comparable height, the differentials in their characters and behaviour had manifested themselves into the evolution of their physiques.

Holmes's constant use of both physical and nervous energy had resulted in a trim and wiry frame that was capable of any degree of exertion and endurance. However, in direct contrast to his brother, many years of sloth and lethargy had resulted in Mycroft's somewhat bulkier stature that was, at times, barely capable of movement at all!

Consequently, it had been easy for me to appreciate the significance of our venture in Bavaria, by virtue of the fact that

Mycroft had taken such unprecedented steps in putting the entire enterprise into motion. His meticulous planning and his logical analysis bore a hereditary hallmark and they both seemed to have been enjoying the process of employing their combined and considerable resources towards reaching the same goal.

Of course, my friend did not have the advantage of his brother's insight, which had resulted in an entirely different set of priorities. As ever, Holmes remained relentless in his pursuit of justice and the absolute truth, whereas Mycroft understood more clearly the power wielded by the Brotherhood and the scope of their ultimate plan. Nevertheless, Holmes's successful procurement of the papers had brought both brothers closer to their respective purposes. I sat back breathlessly in my chair while the two of them decided what the best course of action should be going forward. They were both convinced that Gruner had as much to fear from his associates as he had from the Bavarian police, and the three of us.

There was now as little point in our remaining in Bavaria as there was for Gruner to have done so. Consequently, an early return to London was decided upon and we stoked up the fire before retiring for the night.

'What course of action have you decided upon, assuming our safe return to London, of course?' I found myself asking over our final smokes of the day.

Holmes and his brother seemed uncertain as to which of them should give me my reply, but Holmes finally gave Mycroft the honours with an inviting sweep of his hand.

'First of all, Dr Watson, our safe return to London is not an assumption, it is a certainty. I can assure you that Gruner will not make a move against us until he is assured of his own safety, nor until he has gauged the manner in which we intend to make use of his papers. Do not forget, he had neither the time nor the opportunity to ascertain which of those papers we took or those that we had left behind.

'If there is one thing that we can be certain of, it is the importance that both Gruner and his fellow members of the Brotherhood attach to them. Therefore, I fully intend to give my undivided attention to the task of analysing them without a moment's delay. I can best do so in a place of total isolation and relative safety. Therefore, upon my return, I fully intend to resign from my position within the government and relinquish my membership of the Diogenes Club before retiring to my bolthole in the central Highlands, a secluded old drover's lodge not far from Inverness.

'Upon my arrival, I shall maintain a line of communication with London and inform you of my discoveries as and when I have made them. You should not forget that, although I shall be giving up those illustrious appointments, many of my auxiliaries will always lend their loyalty and considerable abilities to my cause. As ever, Sherlock,' he concluded, addressing my friend directly, 'I shall leave the more energetic aspects of the investigation in your more than capable hands!'

'For you to give up such cherished positions I must conclude that the gravity of these people's intentions are unique in your experience,' Holmes ventured.

'Your conclusions are impeccable, Sherlock,' Mycroft replied gravely, turning down the lantern.

Even before we had the chance to settle down properly, the silence of the lodge was shattered by a series of sharp and urgent knocks upon the front door. I was the first to my feet and I walked gingerly towards the door,my revolver cocked and ready to fire, while Holmes followed closely behind me with his weighted cane raised and poised to strike.

We edged ever closer to the door and I could feel my pulse quicken as I recollected Mycroft's words of dire warning. Could the calculations of a man of such intellect be proved to be so utterly wrong? As I shot back the bolt, I stood away in expectation of the door being thrust violently towards us.

Our anxieties could not have been further from the truth nor our precautions more unnecessary, for the opened door revealed nothing more threatening than the sight of Mycroft's cold and bedraggled agent, Ara Vukovic, trembling uncontrollably before us.

CHAPTER NINE

AN UNEXPECTED COMPANION

My instinctive reaction was to rush towards her and to drape
one of our blankets over her shuddering shoulders. Once I
had guided her over to a fireside chair, I stoked up the dying
embers while Mycroft produced a slender pocket flask that
contained some warming whisky.

Only Holmes appeared to have been unmoved by her
plight, and while Mycroft and I had been busy making
Miss Vukovic more comfortable, Holmes merely stared
contemplatively into her luminous green eyes as if he was
trying to analyse her motives for being there in the first
place.

To my somewhat less cynical mind these seemed to be
rather obvious. Clearly she had fled from the castle with some
urgency, for she was bereft of any outer garments, save for
her brown calfskin boots, and her black silk shirt was clearly
inadequate for the task of protecting her from the harsh
elements outside.

'What happened to you, my dear?' enquired Mycroft
sympathetically.

Miss Vukovic was clearly disturbed by my friend's close attention, for she returned Holmes's penetrative gaze even while she was replying to his brother's question.

'After your hasty departure, the police seemed to decide that I knew, somehow, of your current whereabouts. This surprised me, because I was under the impression that you had taken them into your confidence and had also promised them the prized scalp of a notorious murderer. Was this not so, Herr Holmes?'

'Indeed it was, my dear; however, those damned fools have not only bungled the capture of Baron Gruner, but they have now added to this the insult of harassing one of my agents! I am not surprised that you have been able to evade their attentions so completely,' he said with a smile.

'Neither am I,' Holmes confirmed under his breath, maintaining his intense scrutiny of our guest. However, none of us could decide if his remark was born out of admiration for the young lady, or perhaps from his low opinion of the local police.

I was surprised that Holmes had not yet commented upon the fact that someone who bore such an obviously Croatian name should speak with such a flawless Germanic accent, although I was sure that if that thought had crossed my mind it had certainly crossed his.

'For some reason they did not seem to realise that I am in your employ, Herr Holmes,' Miss Vukovic continued, 'otherwise I am certain that they would not have treated me so roughly.'

'Naturally I could not risk telling them about the lodge or of our intention to use it as our base. I suppose they were trying to locate their missing horses,' Mycroft speculated, although he was obviously embarrassed by the young lady's questioning.

'Actually, it had been the discovery of their missing mounts, and the distraction that it had caused, that gave me the opportunity to escape their attentions. While they argued amongst themselves, I was able to quietly slip away and soon afterwards I managed to lose myself in the forest. However, I still do not understand why they treated me so, given the fact that I work for you.' Mycroft turned away shamefaced as Miss Vukovic continued with her speculation.

'You must try to understand, my dear,' Mycroft finally confessed, 'that I could not be certain of the loyalty of the police, even at this late stage in my plans, and therefore, if this knowledge had been compromised, so too would have been your safety and that of poor old Gabriel.'

'So, in order to preserve the security of your project, you decided to abandon the two of us to our fates? Mine was to be forcibly detained and questioned, whereas Gabriel met with a far graver consequence, all while we were in your service.' The young lady appeared to have been more confused at her shabby treatment than she was angry.

This fact was not lost on Mycroft, who tried to placate her in the only way that he could. 'There is so much more at stake here than you could possibly hope to understand,' he said quietly.

'Nevertheless,' interjected Holmes, 'you have made good your escape and I am certain that my brother has no intention of allowing you to fall into the slippery hands of the police for a second time. Even should they be able to locate you, a likelihood that borders on the implausible, a simple explanation from him would certainly be enough to satisfy them and guarantee your liberty, would you not say, Mycroft? After all, your influence seems to recognise neither borders nor limitations.' Holmes seemed to be enjoying the process of increasing his brother's discomfiture.

Mycroft had been duty bound to concur with my friend's assertions when faced with the prospect of an emotional display from the distraught Miss Vukovic.

'My brother's assurances are not without foundation, my dear, and you can be certain that from this moment on you shall have nothing further to fear from the authorities.'

'As comforting as this pledge surely is,' said she, 'I am more concerned by the potential threat posed by Baron

Gruner and his people. After all, you have stressed on more than one occasion, the power that these people can wield. What is to be my fate, Mr Holmes?' Mycroft was clearly taken aback by the forceful manner with which the young lady had voiced her concerns and he mumbled under his breath as he lit a cigar.

'Naturally my brother was about to propose that you should travel back to London with us under the shield of our protection, Miss Vukovic,' Holmes proposed with a mischievous smile. 'Once there, I am certain that he will have no great difficulty in finding a suitable and secure situation for someone with your singular talents.' Mycroft replaced his monocle that he might verify how serious were his brother's intentions. One glance at my friend was enough to confirm this to the elder Holmes brother and we all readily accepted his proposals, although with differing reactions and emotions. I, of course, was both amazed and surprised by my friend's considerations; Miss Vukovic viewed them with an understandable suspicion, whereas Mycroft accepted them with an obvious and resigned reluctance. Nevertheless, it was universally agreed that we should all try to take some rest before planning and executing the long journey home.

Mycroft's disgruntled mood had not abated by the time we had all awoken on the following morning and he decided to leave the travel arrangements to me and my trusty Bradshaw with a crusty display of indifference. Of course, the extra horses enabled us to return to Hohenschwangau without any great difficulty, but Holmes surprised me again when he gave up his coat to the ill-prepared young woman as we ventured out from the frost-covered lodge. However, the next stage of our journey would prove to be somewhat more problematical.

Our only means of transport from Hohenschwangau to Fussen appeared to be the horse and cart of Peter Kohl the younger, and he was not due to return until the following morning. Although Holmes grunted his frustration at having to endure a delay, secretly I was somewhat relieved, for it afforded us the opportunity to sample the delights and comforts of the Gasthaus Muller once again.

I decided to take full advantage of both, for I had not slept nor eaten properly for nigh on forty-eight hours, and the attractions of a soft bed and some hot food were obvious to all of us save for Sherlock Holmes. His pipe appeared to be the only solace that he sought and the three of us left him to it when we finally retired to our respective rooms.

The following morning we completed a hearty breakfast and awaited the arrival of our cart in fine spirits. Bradshaw indicated a suitable afternoon train from Fussen to Munich and the remainder of our journey appeared to have been a relatively simple matter. Nevertheless, Holmes seemed to be more pensive than usual and I realised that his darting eyes were ceaselessly on their guard for indications of our enemies. Mercifully, his vigilance had been, for now at least, a futile, albeit disturbing, precaution.

We four spent the majority of the relatively short stage of our journey, the slow train back to Munich, in total silence. No doubt we were all formulating our own thoughts and speculations as to the nature of any forthcoming events. Only Mycroft seemed to be satisfied with that which lay ahead, for he spent the entire three-hour trip in the deepest of slumbers.

Holmes decided to navigate his way around the entire train as a means of ensuring our security, and I observed Miss Vukovic fingering her revolver lightly until Holmes returned to our carriage, obviously satisfied with the results of his reconnoitre.

Bradshaw indicated a four-hour disparity between our arrival in Munich and the departure of our train to Paris. Consequently, Mycroft provided the young lady with funds sufficient for her to replace the more urgent items from her wardrobe. No doubt anxious to return Holmes's coat at the earliest possible opportunity, Miss Vukovic accepted this invitation with great enthusiasm and I accompanied her as she raced around from shop to shop in search of the necessary items.

'Herr Doctor, your friend does not appear to trust me, do you not find?' she asked as we made our way back to the station with the laden bags.

She had glided her way around the shops with such speed and efficiency that we still had an hour to spare before our scheduled departure. Consequently, we had slowed our progress to a saunter and her sudden accusation took me off guard. I smiled at her reassuringly and lit a cigarette before offering my reply. Miss Vukovic was certainly not a young lady who was slow in coming forward.

'I can assure you that Mr Holmes has not voiced any concerns about you to me.' I smiled.

'Perhaps not, but you must have noticed how continuously he has stared at me, ever since my dramatic return to the lodge?'

'Under the circumstances, I would suppose that he is understandably wary of any variations to our schedule, and your entrance had certainly been most unexpected,' I offered speculatively.

'Perhaps he is uncertain of the motives of all women, Dr Watson? After all, you have alluded to such a phenomenon in some of your accounts.' This time her perceptiveness managed to stop me in my tracks, for I had not expected a conversation of such a personal nature.

'You have read my chronicles of Holmes's investigations?'

'Of course; his brother has always insisted that they be required reading, if we were to learn anything at all about observation and deduction.'

'Well, Mr Holmes will be delighted, if not a little surprised, to hear that!' I exclaimed with a laugh.

Before she could say another word, I sped away from Miss Vukovic until she was out of sight; such had been my enthusiasm for relating her revelation to my friend. Upon reaching the station, I pulled Holmes to one side and immediately offered him my amused congratulations.

'Hah! Oh Watson, has it not occurred to you that once again you have allowed yourself to be beguiled by the allures and flattery of an attractive young woman?' he suggested with a smile.

'Ah, so you admit at last that you do find Miss Vukovic to be attractive?' I goaded.

'No, not at all, but even I could not have failed to recognise those qualities that you have always found to be so appealing in the fairer sex. By the way, what exactly has become of the young lady in question? I am afraid that your desire to ridicule me at the earliest opportunity has dulled your judgement, Watson. You forget the cloud of threat that is constantly hanging over our heads.' Holmes's unique ability to transform a light-hearted moment into a sombre chastisement rocked me back on my feet and I immediately retraced my steps.

I did not have far to go, as Miss Vukovic had arrived at the station just a moment later, but my embarrassment was further heightened by the look of amusement with which she greeted me. Therefore, my relief upon hearing the final call for our train's departure might be well understood and mercifully the subject was not broached again throughout the entire journey home.

With so many questions remaining unanswered, the prospect of a sixteen-hour train journey presented us with a laborious and frustrating prospect. After a brief diversion in the dining car, we returned to our compartment in a pensive silence. Finally, we were diverted from our sombre malaise when Holmes asked Miss Vukovic to tell us something of her life's history.

Despite Mycroft's return to his recurrent state of slumber, her narration provided Holmes and I with a fascinating tale indeed.

Both of her parents had died when she had been still quite young and, consequently, she had been brought up by her mother's sister in the small coastal town of Lovran. She had supported her aunt by working at the busy fishing port skinning the fish caught there. When not engaged at the port she toiled upon the fields of one of the local farms and as a result she grew up to be a strong and healthy young woman.

When her aunt had passed away, Miss Vukovic moved to the city of Split, where she met and fell in love with the son of an Austrian nobleman. She returned with him to Salzburg, but the petulant heir had soon grown tired of her, as is often the wont of young men of a certain class, and she had now found herself alone and abandoned in a foreign land.

The young nobleman had at least furnished her with a small room, albeit in the poorer part of the city, and she soon learned how to become both resilient and self-sufficient. She stood out from the majority of her wretched and pitiable neighbours by virtue of her striking appearance and stature, so for her to be set upon, when out on the streets at night, became a not uncommon occurrence.

She soon learned how to defend herself and fight back, and it was during one of these fracases that she first came to the attention of one of Mycroft's agents, the very same Gabriel Serban who had died on that fateful night at the castle. It was rare for a woman of such beauty to also possess the ruthless fighting skills that were so often employed in that line of work.

Under Gabriel's tutelage and with Mycroft's wholehearted approval and support, she soon became an invaluable addition to Mycroft's clandestine cohorts and her rapid progress culminated in her crucial role in the raid upon the castle of Neuschwanstein.

'My, my! What a truly remarkable story, and you have undoubtedly experienced enough to satisfy a thousand lifetimes,' I remarked softly. I looked to my friend for confirmation, but found him to be gazing out of the window, bearing all of the hallmarks of indifference.

'Holmes?'

He slowly turned away from his miasmic view of the rolling landscape and his response, through a cloud of tobacco smoke, had been barely audible.

'It was indeed a fine tale, Watson.'

Evidently no other words were to be forthcoming from my inscrutable friend. Miss Vukovic and I exchanged looks of perplexity and we concluded the journey in a stilted and uncomfortable silence.

A wire from Paris had ensured that we were to be met at the station by none other than Dave 'Gunner' King. To say that he appeared to be embarrassed and apologetic would be to understate in the extreme.

'A thousand apologies, Mr 'Olmes. I would never have betrayed your confidence or disregarded your orders under normal circumstances. It just seemed to me that you would have been better off with Dr Watson by your side than without him,' King explained.

Holmes chuckled and slapped the stalwart cabby across the shoulders without even a hint of recrimination.

'My dear fellow, such insubordination should be applauded and not subject to the need of apology. As ever, the presence of Dr Watson was of invaluable and immeasurable benefit. Therefore, I congratulate you upon your perceptive disregard of my instructions!'

A moment later a much-relieved King had loaded our luggage aboard and he was soon driving us towards Baker Street with his customary gusto and total disregard for the laws of physics!

CHAPTER TEN

AN UNEXPECTED VISITOR

A quick examination of my Bradshaw indicated that there would be no further trains to Inverness until the following evening. Naturally this minor inconvenience presented our much put-upon landlady with a major domestic dilemma. It was soon decided that I was to sacrifice my bed for the benefit of Miss Vukovic, while Holmes was to be similarly deprived for the sake of his brother.

'Is it not bad enough that you both disappear for days on end without a word, but now I have to strip down and make up beds, not to mention the extra meals!' Mrs Hudson rubbed her hands together in anticipation of the labours that lay ahead. Nevertheless, there was a trace of relish in her voice as she set about her tasks and the briefest of smiles in response to Holmes's most charming of apologies.

Our arrangements went smoothly enough and soon Holmes and I were settling into our customary chairs in anticipation of a cold and uncomfortable night. As it transpired, a large port soon alleviated my fears of any sleeplessness, but through my closing eyelids I saw Holmes preparing for a long vigil with his pipe. Discomfort caused me to awake several times during the night and on each occasion, I saw that Holmes's position and posture had remained unchanged. I could only speculate upon the thoughts and analysis that were going on within that inscrutable and complex mind, and if I had anticipated any revelations over breakfast on the following morning, I was to be sorely disappointed.

After the breakfast things had been removed by a disgruntled Mrs Hudson, Holmes suggested that Miss Vukovic might travel to Inverness with his brother.

'Are you suggesting that I need the protection of a woman?' Mycroft protested.

'No, not at all; however, to allow a young lady of such singular gifts to remain unemployed would appear to be most profligate and remiss of you. I would rather regard it as an arrangement that provides both of you with mutual benefits.'

'Do I have any say in the matter?' the young lady asked sarcastically.

'Well, of course you do, Miss Vukovic, and if you have an alternative suggestion I should very much like to hear it,' Holmes offered mischievously.

Naturally enough she had none to offer and so, at the appointed time, 'Gunner' King arrived to whisk them off to the station.

Initially Holmes seemed to be quite relaxed about that situation, but I was also left with the uncomfortable feeling that he was as much concerned about keeping the young assassin under his brother's surveillance as he was about Mycroft's safety. My friend maintained his reticent response to every question that I fired at him upon the subject, and I could only speculate as to the cause of his mistrust.

After a day or two we received word of their safe arrival in Inverness and Holmes next turned the energy of his frustrations and impatience to the matter of Mycroft's interpretation of Gruner's papers. For my part, it seemed inconceivable that so vast and complex a matter could be resolved in such a short space of time, but Holmes was not so tolerant.

He was sat upon his chair, all the while trimming down his fingernails with his fine front teeth. He barely offered me a glance or a word, but the atmosphere that his inner tension was creating had become excruciating in the extreme.

'Oh, come along old fellow, you cannot reasonably expect to have received word from your brother just yet. Such matters take time and much analysis, and your brother is a man of a most careful and thorough nature. It is a most fine and crisp autumn morning, so let us put these things out of mind, for a short while at least, and strike out upon a curative brisk walk,' I suggested cheerfully.

Holmes put an end to his clumsy attempt at manicure and eyed me quizzically. He strode over to the fireplace and carefully prepared his first pipe of the day.

'So, Watson, I perceive that you have finally succumbed to the lure of West Hampstead and a certain young actress who has just recently returned there, have you not?' He had been referring to Sophie Sinclair, of course, but I had no intention of admitting to such a thing, despite its validity.

'What an absurd notion, Holmes!' I protested. 'You have allowed your preoccupation with the work of your brother to cloud your judgement, I fear.'

Holmes slowly lit his pipe and then he turned suddenly towards me with his right eyebrow arched accusingly.

'My notion, such as you call it, is based simply and logically upon an assimilation of some fairly obvious observations.' I noticed that Holmes had selected his cherry wood as his pipe of choice, a sure sign to me that he was in a disputatious mood.

I sank down into my chair with a resigned and expectant sigh.

'A brief glance at your breakfast plate was enough to convince me that you had become preoccupied upon a matter other than the satisfaction of your hunger. A large, well smoked kipper is normally your favoured means of breaking your fast, is it not?'

I nodded my affirmation.

'Yet, on this particular morning you have barely completed one half of its consumption. Furthermore, when I see that your paper has suffered barely a fold or a crease, I know that your attention has been drawn elsewhere. A pass behind your shoulders was enough to reveal the excessive use of your favourite cologne and the crispness of your tie knot is irrefutable,' Holmes concluded with a self-satisfied smile.

'It is nothing of the sort, and I am afraid to say that, on this occasion, your conclusions are purely speculative.' I immediately regretted the use of that word and I was in little doubt that Holmes's response, to the very suggestion that he had resorted to guesswork, would be nothing less than vitriolic.

My fears could not have been any more unfounded and to my surprise Holmes began to laugh as he pulled a familiar looking piece of paper from his inside pocket.

'Watson, you really should have taken more care in concealing the wire that you had received from Inspector Lestrade, if your intention had been to keep your romantic rendezvous a secret. I see that Miss Sinclair returned to her rooms only yesterday, so you are certainly wasting very little time I must say!'

'Really Holmes, that wire was addressed to me!' I complained, while I realised that any further objections would now be futile. 'Oh come along, Holmes, you know full well that your indifference to such matters would have provoked an endless stream of chiding and reproach, had I revealed my plans to you,' I explained.

'Hah!' Holmes held the wire above his head in triumph. 'You really should get going, Watson, if you are to avoid the midday rush.' A moment later, with my hat and coat in hand, I rushed towards the station, leaving Holmes to his pipe.

Throughout the entire journey to West Hampstead I had sat on the edge of my seat as I agonised over the type of reception that I might expect to receive upon arriving at Miss Sinclair's rooms. After all, the manner of our last parting had not been under the most auspicious of circumstances and much had transpired during the intervening period.

Admittedly, despite all that I had recently seen, heard and experienced, my feelings towards her had neither changed nor diminished. Nevertheless, I could not be certain that these were going to be reciprocated and upon leaving the station I delayed my final approach to her building. I smoked a cigarette just around the corner from her front door, so that my uncertainties might not be observed.

To my great relief, I soon realised that these qualms had been totally unfounded, for she had opened the door wearing a delighted smile and there had been the warmest of greetings in those eyes. However, when she had showed me into her sitting room, I was confronted by a sight that shook me to the core.

A smart young man, obviously of a military bearing although dressed in a sharp civilian suit, rose to greet me with a broad smile and an outstretched hand. I had been so dumbstruck by this unexpected development that I had not even had the good grace to take his hand before turning on my heels and making towards the door. I mumbled a form of apology and began to descend the stairs.

'John, where are you going? You really do not understand!' she called.

Under normal circumstances I should have been thrilled to have heard her use my first name at such an early stage of our acquaintance, but embarrassment had been my motivating emotion and I continued on my way down the stairs.

'Perhaps you would stay if I were to tell you that this gentleman is none other than Lieutenant Simon Sinclair, until recently of the Gordon Highlanders, and he is also my dearest brother!' She had projected her voice in the manner that she had been trained to do when upon the stage and it had had the effect of rooting me to the spot.

If I had felt embarrassment a moment before, it had been nothing compared to the discomfiture that I now felt, and I refused to turn my head until I could feel the blood draining away from my face once more. Once I had done so she took me gently by the hand and led me slowly back into her room.

'My dear fellow, you must think me an awful boor and I owe you a thousand apologies for my discourteous behaviour.' This time I had offered Sinclair my hand and he had accepted it wholeheartedly.

'Not at all, Dr Watson, Sophie has told me all about you and it is a privilege to meet you at long last. I have only recently resigned my commission in order to pursue a career in Whitehall, so I assure you that before too long I shall have my own billet and Sophie shall once again be quite alone.' I had been delighted to hear that Miss Sinclair had spoken of me so favourably and the implication of her brother's statement of intent told me that she would not be averse to any future visits of mine, even in her brother's absence.

For the next hour or so Simon Sinclair and I exchanged a countless succession of military anecdotes while his sister busied herself in her small kitchen by preparing tea and scones. I did not take my leave until the early evening, by which time Simon Sinclair and I had become firm friends and I was as assured of Miss Sinclair's affections as any man ever could be.

I arrived back at Baker Street in the best of spirits; however, I was also wary of the fact that any display of my obvious delight at the outcome of my afternoon would likely be met by Holmes's most cynical scowl and disdain. Therefore, I was relieved to find him engaged in the most intense concentration while in the process of interviewing a gruff middle-aged man, whom I could only assume to have been a new client.

CHAPTER ELEVEN

THE ENIGMATIC TALISMAN

Naturally I lost little time in offering my apologies for such an intrusion, but Holmes was having none of it. Without a moment's notice he had flung my notebook and pencil unceremoniously towards me and it had been all that I could do to catch them before they might strike me on the head!

Although the presence of this client had spared me from Holmes's inevitable ridicule and chastisement, it had also been a relief to find my friend occupied upon a matter other than his brother's progress in Scotland. Indeed, such had been his obsession in that regard that he had been turning away clients and potential cases that, under normal circumstances, would have proved to have been irresistible to him. Consequently, I could be assured that the problem now being presented to him had been of a rare and atypical nature, and I sat down with my pencil raised with relish.

'Oh Watson! The very notion of Mr Imrie commencing his narrative in your absence was unthinkable!' Holmes said while also indicating impatiently that I should remove my coat.

'You were so certain of my return at this time?' I asked.

'I know that my Watson's sense of propriety would have prevented him from spending an entire day and evening in the company of a young lady.'

The sound of our new client clearing his throat brought our brief exchange to an immediate conclusion, and Holmes offered him the opportunity to introduce himself once more before outlining the problem that had brought him to our door.

'This is my friend, Dr Watson,' Holmes addressed the gentleman, 'before whom you can speak as freely as before myself.'

'Very well then,' Imrie affirmed while lighting a panatela. 'Gentleman, my name is Percival Imrie, and I can assure you at the outset that neither man nor woman as ever sat before you has been beset by a more perplexing problem than the one that I intend to lay before you now.'

Holmes and I raised stares at the man who had made so bold a claim, and we could see that he was at least sincere in his assertion. Imrie was a man in his mid-fifties, I should say, and despite his bluff complexion and rugged features, he possessed a voice that was lighter and more lyrical than one would have expected. Although of a corpulent build, Imrie carried it well; his grey hair had grown wispy in places and his spectacles seemed to be hardly adequate, as he appeared to have a perpetual squint.

'That, Mr Imrie, remains to be seen and for us to judge. Please try to be somewhat less dramatic when you are actually making your statement, as I am really only interested in the bare facts. For example, I can see from the muscular development of your hands and lower arms, and from your complexion, that you have spent much of your life working out of doors in an industrial capacity, probably as a farmer.'

In answer to Imrie's gasp of incredulity, Holmes explained:

'There are both teeth and claw marks up and down your cane that could have only come from those of a Border Collie. However, either great success in your industry or a considerable inheritance has seen a remarkable upturn in your fortunes of late, as your comfortable corpulence and elegant suit readily attest to. I would suggest inheritance,' Holmes concluded with a self-satisfied smile. 'for I cannot imagine many farms that could finance a visit to Number One Saville Row.'

Imrie's dumfounded silence was enough to satisfy Holmes that each one of his conclusions had indeed been accurate. However, I still required further explanation.

'Holmes, although I follow your reasoning, up to a point, I cannot for the life of me understand how you can pinpoint the exact location of Mr Imrie's tailor so accurately or the timing of his new-found wealth.'

'I have made a small study of yarns and stitching and I can assure you, Watson, that nobody rolls a lapel and applies such bold stitching quite like Number One Saville Row. I also happen to know that a suit from those premises requires many fittings over a number of weeks, and I can assure you that their initial measurement of Mr Imrie's waist was more accurate than the current strain on his waistband would lead one to believe.'

'Now steady on, Mr Holmes!' Imrie obviously felt slighted and was left uncomfortable by Holmes's rather personal observation and he attempted to hide the offending garment by pulling his jacket across his stout frame, somewhat unsuccessfully. However, once his embarrassment had abated, Imrie conceded each one of Holmes's deductions with both admiration and humility.

'Now please, Mr Imrie, outline to us in exact detail the nature of this most exceptional problem of yours, while keeping the hyperbole to the barest minimum.' Without a moment's hesitation, Imrie relit his cigar and began.

'I had not been the only beneficiary of our Great Aunt Martha's will and testament, and my brother George, for whom I have always had the highest regard, made use of his share in a manner that took him upon a totally different direction and location to my own.

'While I had expanded and enhanced our late parent's holding in Norfolk to the point whereby its success and resources allows me a more than comfortable lifestyle, George abandoned a life on the land in favour of an investment in the ever-expanding shipping industry in Liverpool. I must say that it was a decision that he has never once regretted and his enterprise and foresight have seen him become a very wealthy man in his own right.

'Despite our dissimilar lifestyles, George and I have always remained on the very best of terms and since we have both chosen to maintain our bachelor status, we are indeed the only family that either one of us possesses. Consequently, at this time of year, we have maintained the convention of exchanging letters, in which we inform the other of the events and our thoughts of the past year, together with a token festive gift.' At this point Imrie paused and he eyed Holmes in a manner that suggested that my friend would not view his next statement in a favourable light. The reason for this would soon become apparent.

'Now I have to tell you about the miniature bust of the Empress Agrippinilla and the importance that my brother attaches to it . . .' Holmes halted the farmer in his tracks by raising his right hand and arching his left eyebrow. Naturally, I understood the reason for this, because Holmes possessed as little knowledge of ancient history as he did of more current political events.

'Agrippinilla was both the wife of the Emperor Claudius and the mother of the notorious Nero,' Imrie explained. 'Being the great granddaughter of the great Augustus, she commanded huge respect and adulation from the Roman populace and, consequently, Nero became so jealous of this fact that he actually began to plot against the life of his own mother! Finally, once all attempts at a more subtle approach to this ambition had resulted in embarrassing failure, he simply despatched some trusted guards to carry out the deed.'

'Mr Imrie, I trust that this fascinating tale has some actual bearing upon the matter at hand?' My friend was clearly becoming exasperated by our client's laborious manner and he embellished the word 'fascinating' with a liberal dose of sarcasm.

'Oh indeed it has, Mr Holmes,' Imrie confirmed, and he now made a conscious effort at accelerating his narrative. 'Nero did not survive his mother by many years: his debauchery and cruelty finally enraged the Senate and the people of Rome to such an extent that he was left with no alternative other than to take his own life, thereby saving himself from the ignominy of arrest and execution.

'It was said at the time that at the very moment of Nero's death, the face upon this miniature bust of his mother immediately broke into a strange and enigmatic smile . . .'

'Mr Imrie, please!' Holmes suddenly leapt up from his chair and strode over to the window, ignoring Imrie's perplexity at having been interrupted once again. 'Had I desired to hear such a fanciful tale I could have quite simply referred to the brothers Grimm. Good day, Mr Imrie!' Holmes dismissed the man with a wave of his arm and without even turning to face him.

To his credit, however, Imrie stood his ground.

'Mr Holmes, I can understand your reluctance to listen further and I can assure you that, had it not been for the importance that my brother attaches to it, I should have given this legend no credence either, much less inconvenience you with its repetition. However, the fact remains that upon hearing of the fable of the bust, my brother henceforth refused to let the repulsive object out of his sight.' Holmes finally relented and he returned to his chair, his long fingers forming a steeple beneath his chin.

'From that moment on,' Imrie continued, 'the bust of Agrippinilla became George's most treasured possession, his talisman, in fact, and he came to believe, beyond question, that it shielded him from all harm. When he went outdoors, regardless of which garment he happened to be wearing, the talisman would be in one of his pockets. When he went to bed at night, the talisman would be resting upon his bedside table providing George with the comfort of its protective and watchful gaze. Indeed, so deep-rooted had become his belief in its power that on the one occasion when he had temporarily misplaced it, his servants informed me that he went into a blind panic and could not be consoled until his valet found the bust perched upon the edge of the bathroom sink.'

'Do you know of any dangers from which your brother might have felt threatened?' I asked. 'After all, his actions and superstitions are those of a nervous and vulnerable man.'

'There are none that I know of. By all accounts, he does not have an enemy in the world and he is universally well regarded both within his industry and amongst his large social circle. I can only imagine that a demon that has remained dormant within his subconscious all these years has somehow resurfaced and set off this uncharacteristic paranoia. His talisman seems to be the only thing that can placate it.'

'Therefore,' ventured Holmes, 'you seek my advice and consultation as to why your brother should send such a venerated object to you as this year's Christmas gift, do you not?'

'Indeed I do, Mr Holmes!' Imrie exclaimed incredulously, 'But how, in the name of good fortune, did you know that?'

Holmes laughed out loud at Imrie's display of amazement, so I volunteered an answer on his behalf.

'The edge of a small buff envelope is protruding from your top pocket, Mr Imrie, and there is also a small circular distortion in the cloth of your jacket that belies the cut of such a well-made suit.' Imrie blushed at such an obvious omission and he slowly removed the package from his pocket.

'Oh Watson, this is most excellent work!' Holmes exclaimed. 'Clearly if one stands too close to the flame of genius it is inevitable that one will become slightly singed.'

I could not help but laugh out loud at my friend's unabashed egotism, a fault which he often displayed, but regarding which he remained in blissful ignorance.

'Well, I suppose I am meant to receive this as some kind of a distorted compliment?' said I.

'You should know full well by now,' said he, 'that I regard a compliment as much of a deviation from the truth as an insult, Watson. You may take it as you will, but I can assure you that I meant it as nothing of the sort.' After this short rebuke, Holmes turned his attention to our client once more.

Imrie offered him the envelope, but Holmes continued instead with his questioning of the portly client.

'Mr Imrie, do you happen to know the exact circumstances by which your brother came to be in possession of this object, and the means by which he came to learn of its unique powers?'

'As far as I understand it, George was coming towards the end of his 'Grand Tour' in Rome where he was accosted by a group of Gypsy beggars as he was making his way through the Forum. He parted with a few Lire but, as he was turning towards the Capitoline Museums, he felt a thin but surprisingly strong hand upon his shoulder. He turned to find an ancient Gypsy woman grinning up at him and in her hand she held the bust in question. It was she who had told him the story of Agrippinilla and the effect that the talisman had had upon the lives of all who had owned it previously.

'The Gypsy refused any further payment as she pressed it into my brother's reluctant palm and before George could offer protest and return it to her, the aged crone had disappeared into a throng of her fellow beggars. George placed it into his pocket and thought nothing further of it until he had returned home and his valet found it lying at the bottom of his trunk. That night my brother went to play bridge at his club and such had been his good fortune at the table, that from that moment on he became a firm believer in the potency of the talisman. It has been in his possession ever since.'

'Until now, of course!' I confirmed excitedly.

Holmes ignored my emotional outburst and sat there gently stroking his chin while lost in the deepest contemplation.

'Can you think of any reason for your brother's decision to give up the talisman at this particular time?' Holmes asked quietly and then in response to Imrie's slowly shaking head, enquired; 'Was there anything unusual within his letter that might provide an indication?'

'Perhaps he has simply decided to share his good fortune with his brother?' I suggested.

'No, no, no, no.' This time it was Holmes who shook his head and he finally accepted the envelope from Imrie's outstretched hand. To my surprise, Holmes seemed to be more interested in the envelope than its contents and he tossed the talisman over to me while he brought out his smallest glass.

The bust of Agrippinilla was indeed a most unique and remarkable object. Despite its great age, the smooth marble surface of the talisman remained unblemished and flawless. The engraving had lost none of its depth and clarity, and as one gazed at its features, it became impossible to deny the fact that its strange triumphal smile had achieved a form of animation.

Holmes broke in upon my reverie with an exclamation of both surprise and exasperation.

'Mr Imrie, did you not find it at all strange, or at the least worthy of mention, to discover that there is no postage mark upon the stamp?'

The look of surprise upon Imrie's portly face seemed to indicate that he had not noticed that vital fact.

'Did you not even know that your brother was in London, for that could be the only explanation for the absence of the mark?' Holmes asked.

'No sir, I did not.'

'This matter becomes more opaque by the second,' Holmes stated thoughtfully. He raised his glass to the envelope and became quite excited once he had discovered a watermark within it.

'The quality of the stationary indicates an above average, medium sized hotel, but the mark is unmistakable. Your brother has surely taken residence at "Brown's." Mr Imrie, I am afraid that I must ask you for the letter.'

Imrie reluctantly handed this over, while complaining that it contained nothing of note and that its contents were of a somewhat personal nature.

Holmes read the sheets with a disinterested haste, until he came to a short passage that seemed to arouse his interest.

'I apologise, Mr Imrie, but you must understand that I would not have asked this of you had it not been of the utmost importance.'

'You have found something indicative?' I asked.

Holmes took the sheet over to our client and thrust his finger upon the paragraph in question.

'Why,' said he, 'when everything in his life seemed to be set so fair, would your brother suddenly have considered himself not worthy enough to retain custodianship of his most prized possession?'

Imrie twisted uncomfortably in his seat and could not bring himself to look at my friend directly.

'I can only imagine that he is referring to the matter of the steamship *Gunter*.'

'Go on,' Holmes insisted.

'For months he had been wracked with guilt over the warning that he had received from his chief engineer over the *Gunter*'s potential lack of seaworthiness. The engineer had not been convinced that the *Gunter*'s hull, although sound, would be able to withstand the stress exerted by an extreme storm. However, his German clients were putting my brother under extreme pressure for a prompt delivery, and he had neither the time nor the resources to strengthen the hull further. He faced certain financial ruin were the *Gunter* not delivered on time and he allowed its launch, despite his engineer's most dire warning.'

Imrie was visibly shamed by his brother's deceit and recklessness, and he sank back into his chair.

'I can see no mention of the *Gunter* in here,' Holmes informed our client, tapping the paper.

'He only mentioned it briefly in his previous letter.'

'In that case, something else must have occurred, during the intervening period, which has prompted his unheralded journey to London.' Holmes's speculative voice tailed away as he dwelt upon the significance of his previous statement.

'I think I may have it!' I suddenly exclaimed, upon recollecting a column from within a recent, well-thumbed morning newspaper.

Holmes suddenly sprang from his chair, gathered up each one of Imrie's items, and then pulled on his overcoat as he strode purposely to the door. He had barely afforded the column a second glance.

ALL HANDS LOST IN STORM

'There is not a moment to lose!' Holmes called over his shoulder and we followed in his wake as he frantically tried to hail the first available hansom.

Holmes did not offer a single word of explanation as we made a laboriously slow passage towards our intended destination, but I was in little doubt that we were heading towards Brown's Hotel. I could see from my friend's steely gaze that he considered our prompt arrival there as being a matter of the greatest moment. I was immediately consumed with a wave of my own misgivings, and I could not even bare to speculate as to Imrie's own state of mind.

Our first fears had been realised before we had even alighted from our cab, for there, pulled up outside of the small, elegant but discreet building that was Brown's, was the all too familiar sight of a police wagon. Holmes drew sighs of astonishment and indignation from the gathering crowds as he pushed his way through them, and he needed no directions to George Imrie's room, for the route was lined with constables, all stood to attention. In the background could be heard the plaintive cries for discretion from the hotel's dapper little manager, but these were in vain.

To our mutual surprise, we were greeted at the door to Imrie's room by the familiar sight of our old friend, Inspector Lanner of Scotland Yard.

'Good heavens, Mr Holmes,' exclaimed Lanner, 'I certainly did not expect to see you here today!'

'Nor I you, Inspector; however, your presence certainly confirms my worst fears for the well-being of Mr George Imrie.'

Lanner shook his head sombrely.

'It is indeed a sorry business, Mr Holmes, although I fail to see how you have come to hear of this tragedy so soon after its occurrence.' The inspector glanced at Imrie. 'Who might this other gentleman be?'

'This is Mr Imrie's brother, Mr Percival Imrie. It was he who first brought this matter to my attention. I suggest that we three examine the room alone until we are more certain of our facts. Perhaps a chair might be found for Mr Imrie?' Holmes suggested, surprisingly conscious of the fact that our client might be unduly distressed by whatever was awaiting us within the room.

At once a constable helped our shaken client into a chair in the corridor, before taking up a position that secured the door from any potential observers. Meanwhile, Holmes, Inspector Lanner and I stepped inside the room. The awful scene that now confronted us bore an uncanny resemblance to the one that we had encountered in Sutton's room, during our investigation into that most singular Brook Street affair.[11] That grotesque feeling of déjà vu was compounded by the fact that Inspector Lanner had been present on that occasion as well!

We closed the door silently behind us and then stared in awe as we beheld a sight that was so calamitous and finite. The silence was only broken by the sound of the ship's rope being slowly stretched by Imrie's weight as he swung gently back and forth, in the manner of a macabre pendulum.

George Imrie had been a paler and less robust version of his brother, no doubt a reflection of his unhealthier

---

[11]   From 'The Adventure of the Red-Headed League' by Sir A.C.D.

lifestyle, although now his features were contorted by the dire circumstances of his death. His lifeless form was hanging by the neck from a thick noose, no doubt fashioned from one of his anchor ropes, which was attached to an enormous chandelier rose in the centre of the ceiling. A sturdy oak occasional table was lying on its side close by, indicating that it had recently been kicked away with force.

'Surely the poor devil can be brought down and removed, before we begin to examine the room?' I asked indignantly as Holmes began to analyse the table.

'The hotel manager had requested that we delay his removal until he could be certain that it was to be undertaken outside of the public gaze,' Lanner explained. However, the inspector was now decided that he had pandered to the hotel's desire for discretion for long enough, and he immediately called for four bearers to carry out the morbid and sacred deed.

We had hoped against hope that Holmes's conclusions would mirror those that he had reached in Brook Street, for the idea that his brother had taken his own life would be harder for Percival to bear than any other form of death.

Holmes began his inspection with the mark on the table and then turned his attention towards the chandelier, which had been laid carefully upon the floor in preparation for the fixing of the rope. My friend certainly possessed above average strength, but I could tell by the ease with which he had lifted the ornate light fitting that Imrie too would also have been capable of such a feat.

The sight of Holmes slithering around on the floor with his glass in hand, was one with which I was not entirely unfamiliar. Lanner and I observed him with a watchful gaze as my friend moved from footprint to footprint without a moment's pause. His impassive expression left me in little doubt that the results of each examination were the same on each occasion. He examined the windows and the door fittings with equal care, but when he finally put the glass away it was not with his usual swagger of triumph.

'Inspector Lanner,' Holmes asked suddenly, 'under what circumstance was Mr Imrie discovered and by whom?'

'One of the maids had been trying to change his bed linen all day, but she was repeatedly denied access to do so by Imrie's gruff refusal to open his door. Finally, when her attempts, much later on in the day, were met by an ominous silence and a locked door, she called upon the house manager, who then despatched a burly porter to force the lock. Imrie was found exactly as you see him now, Mr Holmes.'

'Is there any hope,' Lanner continued with little conviction in his voice, 'that your examinations have revealed a conclusion that might differ to our own? Have you discovered a clue that might have eluded us?'

'You have concluded a suicide no doubt?' Holmes asked rhetorically, and Inspector Lanner responded with a solemn nod of his head.

'Well then, Inspector, I have to inform you that I have found nothing with which I might negate your theory. There are no indications that a third party might have gained access to the room, save, of course, for the porter and the maid. The windows are all locked securely from the inside, and there are no scratches or marks on them, or upon the door, that might have told me otherwise. The only visible footprints are those of Mr Imrie, save for the stampede of regulation boots which you have allowed to almost obliterate all of the relevant traces!' As he explained his findings, Holmes went to great pains in indicating each one of them to us in turn.

'The abrasion upon the table was undoubtedly made by Imrie's shoes and, upon further investigation, I am certain that you will discover that the rope came from one of Mr George Imrie's own ships.' Holmes clearly took no great pleasure in pronouncing his conclusions and I was certain that he would next ask me to break the news to Percival, while he completed his report to Inspector Lanner.

I was spared from having to carry out this sorry and thankless task by Percival Imrie himself, who had appeared at the doorway and subsequently overheard each one of my friend's damning deductions. Imrie refused our attempts at consolation and support, and seemed to accept his brother's fate as one who had long been harbouring a resigned premonition.

'Mr Imrie, you should not chastise your brother's memory too much, for although his financial plight appears to have forced him to a decision that was both reckless and irresponsible, an inherent sense of honour would not allow him to profit from the tragic fate of others.' It was obvious that Imrie found no comfort in Holmes's words, and he allowed himself to be led silently away by one of Lanner's more sympathetic constables.

Once Lanner had thanked us for our contribution, Holmes and I made our way back to our cab. To my surprise, Holmes asked the driver to divert our journey by way of the Victoria Embankment.

'As you know, Watson, I have always extolled the virtues of logic over those actions born of emotion, for logic is the purest form of truth, and the truth, no matter how unpalatable, should never be equated to negativity. Nevertheless, I can now perceive and understand the source of that association.' I could find no words of response to Holmes's most singular of statements and we continued on to the river in silence.

As he climbed down from the cab, Holmes invited me to join him by the river's edge. The grey, swirling mass of icy water was pounding relentlessly into the impenetrable wall beneath us, the furious waves driven on by the day's highest tide and a merciless December wind.

Holmes reached into his inside pocket and I was surprised to see that he was clutching the enigmatic talisman.

'Believe me, Watson, when I tell you that there is no force on heaven or earth that can determine a man's destiny with more certainty than his own free will.'

With his words ringing out above the sounds of the elemental turbulence, Holmes pulled back his right arm as if he was about to launch a javelin and hurled the bust of

Agrippinilla into the heart of the maelstrom. Such was the force of his throw that the talisman sank beneath the waves at a point equidistant from both sides of the river.

Holmes hurried back to the cab, satisfied that the malevolent power of the bust had been destroyed forever, and I was certain that his entire focus would now be centred on the findings and communication of his brother. This had been confirmed to me by Holmes's steadfast refusal to dwell or reflect upon the affair of the Imrie brothers for even another moment, and we proceeded to Baker Street in silence.

CHAPTER TWELVE

THE AUTHOR AND THE BANKER

It was indeed fortunate for all concerned that the wait for Mycroft's letter proved to be a brief one.

All too often in the past, Holmes's impatience and its associated anxiety had created an atmosphere in our rooms that had been nothing less than traumatic. Consequently, my relief upon finding a large buff envelope sitting unopened upon our dining table the following morning might be well understood.

Most surprisingly, Holmes had joined me in consuming a large plate of devilled kidneys and curried eggs, but he had paled at the thought of embarking upon a shopping expedition at the behest of our landlady, who was most anxious to put her plans for the imminent Christmas celebrations into place. Thus, when I eventually returned to our rooms, I had been encumbered beneath a load consisting of wreaths of holly, various baking ingredients, and a large plump goose.

I left these items in the eager hands of Mrs Hudson and, although I had been gratified upon seeing the envelope from Mycroft sitting there upon our table, I had been equally surprised to note that it had remained unopened. Holmes was undoubtedly aware of its arrival, but had chosen to await my return before deciding to delve into its contents. He sat there staring intently at his brother's communication, as if his intense scrutiny would somehow reveal its contents. I could not imagine the reason for Holmes's strange behaviour, but I could only assume that he felt apprehensive at the thought of the work, adventures, and dangers of the last few months culminating with the arrival of so unremarkable an object.

'Well, I must say, the thermometer has certainly dived by several degrees and I would not be a bit surprised if we were to see a flake or two of snow before the day is out.' I pronounced, while rubbing my grateful hands together in front of our bright, cheery fire. 'Mercifully, Mrs Hudson appears to be satisfied with my purchases, and no doubt she will appear to hang up the garlands before too long.'

Holmes merely grunted his acknowledgement and continued with his silent, taciturn study.

'Oh, for heaven's sake, Holmes, would you like me to open it for you?' I offered impatiently while picking up the letter opener. Holmes nodded silently and he began filling his old clay pipe from the Persian slipper. Only once he had drawn deeply upon the pungent tobacco did he begin to display any real interest in the reams of paper that I had laid before him upon the table.

'Well, Watson, my brother has certainly been most industrious within his Highland hideaway! Perhaps our long journey is finally coming to a conclusion?'

'Would you like me to look through these for you?' I offered, knowing all too well of my friend's aversion to paperwork of any sort.

'If you would be so kind; I am sure that much of his communiqué will be full of dull irrelevances.' With that, Holmes turned away from me and turned his attention towards the gathering snow clouds outside our windows. He pulled his favourite blanket around his shoulders and maintained a stoic vigil until I had announced to him that I had concluded my studies.

This undertaking was no simple task. For one thing, Mycroft's handwriting was, at best, casual and ungainly, and, at times, barely legible at all! Besides which, I had to reduce his work into a précis, but with enough clarity to satisfy Holmes's desire for bare and precise detail.

Mycroft's letter began as follows:

My dear boy,

I hope this letter finds both you and Dr Watson well.

Miss Vukovic and I are finding the bracing Highland atmosphere to be most agreeable and beneficial, and I must confess that she is settling in well enough under the circumstances. Winter has come early to this Northerly outpost and the snow already lays thick upon the moorlands and the lochs. Miss Vukovic is certainly an amiable enough, if a somewhat standoffish, companion, and I find a certain assurance in the fact that she is constantly cleaning and maintaining her weapons. Nevertheless, one hopes that she is not called upon to use them in any other capacity any time soon.

At this point I made a mental note that I should exclude this opening paragraph from my final presentation to Holmes. However, Mycroft soon turned his attention towards the matter of Baron Gruner and the fact that he remained still very much at large.

I am sorry to have to inform you that our friend Baron Gruner has proved to be a most evasive and resourceful opponent, and he can now best be described as a primed loose cannon. My people were able to pick up his trail shortly after the incident at the castle; after all, the description of Gruner and his daughter could hardly be described as nondescript. Nevertheless, despite my people's intense but discreet observation upon their arrival to these shores, the Gruners slipped through our ring of scrutiny and remain at large and as dangerous as ever.

I am sure that I do not need to remind you that he will be hell-bent on reclaiming his papers and seeking a terrible retribution. Whether or not he decides to begin his search in London or has somehow established my location here in Scotland, I cannot tell, but I assure you both that we shall be maintaining a constant vigilance and would advise that you take similar precautions.

A chill ran through me at these words; although I had no real need of being reminded of Gruner's mortal threat. Nevertheless, I decided that this last paragraph should not be excluded from my summation to Holmes. All the while he had remained oblivious to my reaction and his pipe was excreting a constant flume of smoke as he stared out of the frozen window.

'I trust that my brother and Miss Vukovic are both well?' he asked with a forced nonchalance, without turning towards me as he did so. I confirmed their good health and then continued to read further.

Mycroft now turned his attention to the matter of Gruner's papers and it was all that I could do to contain my emotions as I digested his revelations. The remainder of Mycroft's discourse was both loquacious and complex, so for the sake of clarity I have decided to set out here my own version of Mycroft's interpretation. Equally, for the sake of discretion and prudence, I have omitted the names of some of the leading players in this most salient of dramas.

Unfortunately, because of the extreme conditions under which he had been operating, Holmes had removed the papers at random, with neither a thought of their chronology nor their contents. As a consequence of this, the task that Mycroft had undertaken had proven to be a nigh on impossible one. I felt grateful for this, from a personal and selfish viewpoint, for if the papers had been more complete I should, in all probability, had been reading through them for a week!

If there had been one underlying facet from the very beginning of our odyssey of discovery, the dramatic intrusion of that flamboyant Bedouin, it was the feeling that Holmes and I were only ever scratching the surface of whatever it was that lay beneath. Admittedly, the mysteries with which Gruner had attempted to lure us to our doom had all culminated with our being able to halt his plans in their tracks. Nevertheless, the further we delved into the Brotherhood and their campaign, the less it seemed that Gruner had been a major influence and that our intervention at the castle had been but a minor inconvenience.

As I read on, it soon became obvious that murderous barristers, corrupt coroners, even the revelation of the identity of Jack the Ripper, all paled into insignificance when compared to the broader schemes of the Bavarian Brotherhood as outlined in those papers. Their ultimate goal had been to secure a single, subservient society, governed, or rather, controlled by a finite world order, manipulated by the leading lights in the world of finance and industry. Politicians and the democratic processes that led to their appointment would be nothing more than an impotent facade, tolerated merely to delude and comfort the people who still believed in these false precepts.

The Brotherhood's principle tool was destined to be three calamitous worldwide conflicts, each of which would lead to the development of weapons of previously unknown destructive capabilities and the evolution of intercontinental organisations that would ostensibly ensure a long-lasting, post-war peace. However, these organisations would also be a tool by which ultimate control might be achieved, for which the world's population were supposed to be eternally grateful. Fear, evidently, would be their greatest and most manipulative method.

As I read on, the scope and far-reaching consequences of these plans left me feeling quite breathless, although this was accentuated when I finally began to outline them to my impatient friend. He had been drawn from his position at the window, as I began my preliminary outline, but his excitement and anxieties multiplied to a crescendo when my disposition became more detailed. My description of those devastating new weapons, for example, left him in a state of even greater perplexity than I had been who had read of them first-hand.

'My goodness, Watson! Although Mycroft has occasionally alluded to the development of aeroplanes that are capable of carrying weapons and gigantic armoured vehicles or mobile cannons, these people already appear to be assured of their completion and effectiveness! The third conflict, however, sounds like an implausible piece of hokum. Intercontinental missiles, capable of causing an Armageddon on a worldwide scale — ridiculous! Perhaps these people are not quite as clever as they might have at first appeared. Nevertheless, the prevention of the first two calamities, as unthinkable as they might seem, has to be our primary objective. Unfortunately, our trail goes cold and ultimately terminates with the inevitable demise of Baron Gruner.'

'Are you so certain that this might be achieved?' I asked.

'It has to be achieved, Watson, for the only alternative is that he brings destruction down upon us!' Holmes paused for a moment while he refilled his pipe. His piercing eyes were now aflame as his remarkable faculties tried to assimilate the extraordinary data that they were now being asked to digest.

'Watson, beyond a doubt these are the highest stakes for which we have ever been asked to play. However, by the time that our success, or otherwise, can truly be put to the test, you and I shall have long departed this mortal coil. Be consoled with the knowledge that our efforts will be for posterity and the perpetuation of the race.' Holmes had never been one for avoiding a touch of the dramatic, but I now had to admit that my friend's extraordinary statement of intent had been nothing of the sort. As ever, he was the ultimate pragmatist.

'Do you have a plan, beyond the elimination of Baron Gruner?'

'That is not a plan, Watson, although its accomplishment will prove to be a double-edged sword. As you are only too well aware, each one of our potential leads met with an unfortunate and untimely demise.' He completed his sentence in a somewhat accusing tone; for it is true to say that I had been personally responsible for many of these unfortunately premature deaths.[12]

'I must confess,' he continued, 'that I had expected my brother to have been more forthcoming in supplying us with a hint or two that might have led us upon a different road.'

My friend began to pace the room, pausing every so often to gaze up at the ceiling, as if he were expecting to clutch some inspiration from the ether. While he did so I scanned Mycroft's notes once again, in the hope that some clue might have escaped my attention on the initial reading. Mycroft had made a passing and somewhat cryptic reference to a current and rather successful author, but for our purposes it had hardly seemed to be an inspirational one. Nonetheless, the author's name did sound vaguely familiar to me and I immediately began to search through my burgeoning and creaking bookshelves.

I had no great difficulty in locating this particular tome, for it had only been a recent publication and not yet opened or read. The author had already garnered a reputation for producing thought-provoking and somewhat futuristic work that reflected his socialist political viewpoints. Controversial work, certainly, but it was also hugely popular with the public. Holmes became surprisingly animated when I brought this reference to his attention, and he immediately curtailed his tour around our room.

'Despite its apparently casual insertion, Mycroft must have attached great importance to this book for him to have included its mention at all.' With an impatient gesture, Holmes invited me to carry out a scrutiny of the pages.

The relevant passages were all included in the early chapters of the book, which I immediate passed across to Holmes once I had located them. Sure enough, there was clear reference to the first conflict, which took place during

---

[12] From 'The Four-Handed Game' by P.D.G.

the second decade of the next century, and a second world wide war that resulted in the most horrific and inhumane of consequences. War planes of such, hitherto, unimaginable power and enormous armoured machines that had even attained great speed by the time of the second conflict, were all clearly described within those pages.

Holmes rubbed his prominent chin thoughtfully while he considered the ramifications of my unexpected discovery.

'So, Watson, our author friend is either a prominent member of the Brotherhood, is on intimate terms with one, or has achieved a most fortuitous moment of inspiration. If either of the first two possibilities is the correct one, then this is a gentleman with whom we simply have to meet.' My friend flicked through the book's front pages until he had found the name and location of its publishers.

'I think a visit to The Strand might be in order, Watson,' Holmes suggested.

'I trust that you do not intend to take any further action during my absence?' I asked hopefully.

'I assure you, Watson, that I have no other plans than to simply sit here and to smoke,' Holmes promised, and, as if to confirm his pledge, he began to fill his pipe once more as I made way to the door.

* * *

Thanks to the cooperation of a young secretary, who had proven to be rather susceptible to some of my most charming flattery, I had no great difficulty in achieving my objective. I returned to Baker Street within two hours and discovered that my friend had been as good as his word. Our room had become entombed within a dense haze of smoke and there had been no indication that Holmes had left his chair even the once. Furthermore, according to the testimony of Mrs Hudson, he had not even raised a word of objection when she had invaded his sanctuary in order to hang up our festive garlands of holly.

'I must say, Watson, you have done extraordinarily well,' Holmes said, and once I had shown him the author's address, he despatched Mrs Hudson to engage the services of Dave 'Gunner' King without a moment's delay. Upon the stalwart cabby's arrival, I snatched up my copy of the author's book while Holmes hurriedly gathered together all of Mycroft's papers and stuffed them into his coat pockets before he careered down the stairs behind me.

Despite the length of the journey to Woking in Surrey, King had been rather taken with the idea of shaking away the cobwebs of the smoke-filled metropolis and instead making a leisurely progress through the delightful, but frosty, Surrey landscapes.

The writer had been in a temporary occupancy of a surprisingly modest villa that was bordered by an inharmonious and well employed freight railway line on one side and a small overgrown canal on the other. Each had been dusted by the slow-melting frost, and the villa's short chimneystack was churning out a continuous flume of coal smoke. On such a singularly bitter day, it was indeed a most welcome sight!

Holmes and I stepped down from King's cab with not a little trepidation. After all, we were not even assured of the presence of the object of our curiosity, much less the nature of the reception that two unannounced guests might receive. We looked back to our driver who was fortifying himself for a long cold wait with an extra blanket, which he had pulled out from under his seat, and a small flask which, in all probability, contained a substance of a far greater warmth.

We pulled up our coat collars against the chill air and stepped across the road. The front door was opened to us by a robust young housemaid who boasted bright red cheeks and a permanent scowl. The door stood ajar only as far as the steel security chain allowed, and the young housemaid certainly showed no intention of removing the chain. Holmes and I passed her our cards and she reluctantly agreed to seek her master's advice before defiantly closing the door upon us once more.

We stood for a moment or two in silence, before the chain was finally released and the door was flung wide open as a conciliatory and welcoming gesture.

'Gentlemen, I must offer a thousand apologies to you both! Please step inside at once before you freeze!'

This time we had been greeted by an earnest young man in his early thirties. His cheerful countenance belied the intensity in his eyes that told much of the ideological nature of his work. He was dressed in a light grey tweed suit; his brown hair had been parted and swept across from a point immediately above his left ear, and he sported a most resplendent moustache.

'Naturally I recognised your names at once, but you must understand that the undeserved and unexpected success of my recent works, together with the radical nature of some of the ideas that I propound, have made our residencies, even one as temporary as this one, a target for fans and opponents alike. Therefore, you should not chastise poor Alice for her brusqueness, for she was merely carrying out our bidding. Perhaps a tray of tea and muffins would go a small way towards appeasing your ire?'

Holmes and I readily accepted this most eloquent apology with deep bows and young Alice cheerily made her way to the kitchen to prepare her peace offering.

'Alice appears to be quite happy with her duties,' I observed.

'Indeed she is, Dr Watson, for in this household her position is neither deemed nor treated as a subservient one. Indeed, had my dear wife been present today, she would have, in all probability, prepared the tray herself.'

The author led us through to a small but comfortable sitting room that boasted a stunning view of the surrounding landscape. The walls were lined with bookcases that held a chaotic abundance of books, as one would have expected, and an enormous Christmas tree buckled beneath its load of baubles, holly and candy treats.

'Mr Dickens and Prince Albert certainly had much to answer for,' our host chuckled when he saw our eyes lured towards the resplendent decorations.

As was his habit, Holmes circumnavigated the room, his keen eyes taking in every minute detail, as if he was searching for clues even then. He had hardly acknowledged the author's presence until our tea tray had arrived and we three gathered around an occasional table close to the fire.

'Is it not unusual to have so large a tree in a household with no children present?' Holmes asked before sipping from his cup.

'My wife and I have not been married that long, Mr Holmes. As yet, we have not been blessed with the gift of a child, but the tree gives us hope. However, I fail to see how you would have come to know of her barren status.'

'The tree decorations are of quite a neutral nature, and I have failed to notice those brightly wrapped gifts and stockings that one might have expected to see beneath the tree on the night before Christmas,' Holmes explained before asking our host for permission to smoke.

'Gentlemen, as welcome as a visit from two such celebrated guests surely is, I believe that an explanation for such an unexpected delight might now be due to me. I am certain that I have not been involved in any crime or wrongdoing that I am aware of.'

Holmes leant across and indicated that I might now bring out my copy of our host's book and explain its relevance to our purpose.

'I assure you that our inquiries are not related to any crime, but more to the contents of this, your latest novel. We have noticed that you foresee a future when the air will be full of powerful, flying war machines, and battlefields consumed by huge, armoured battle engines that will be capable of causing terrible devastation. We need to know how it was that you came to reach such awful predictions of our future.'

The author emitted a deep sigh and sank back into his chair. His fingers toyed with the ends of his moustache while he deliberated upon a response to my inquiry, and he then sat forward again, once he had made up his mind.

'It is a most singular inquiry gentlemen, especially since my other readers have all taken it for granted that my creations are nothing more, nor less, than the products of my fertile imagination. I sense, however, that you have an altogether different notion.'

'Indeed, sir, your assumption is a correct one,' I confirmed, although with immediate regret, for my friend's irritation was not well disguised.

With obvious impatience, Holmes pulled the papers out from his pockets and laid them down in an untidy bundle upon the table in front of him.

'There is clearly now no need for me to circumnavigate around the issue,' Holmes declared. 'These documents were appropriated from an isolated and secure establishment in Central Europe, and their removal required a most considerable risk and a still heavier cost. They contain plans for a potential future and it is one that would affect all four corners of the globe. Obviously, their importance cannot be over emphasised—'

'Why are you telling me all of this, Mr Holmes?' the author interrupted my friend in some bewilderment.

'I mention this fact because these plans include the use of some of the futuristic weapons that you have described in your book!' Holmes raised his voice in a most accusing tone and he slammed the papers with his palm as he did so.

The author started up from his chair and glared down at my friend as if he had been greatly affronted.

'Do you actually believe that the contents of my book somehow implicate me in these grandiose plans for some grotesque, projected future? By whose authority are you here today, accusing me in my own home? The police?' This time it was the author's turn to bring his hand down with force upon the papers.

'I assure you that we are here under a far greater authority than the regular police force. No accusation has been made, rather the hope that you might be able to offer a logical explanation for this most singular string of coincidences. Undoubtedly, your refusal to do so would throw a different perspective over this entire matter.' Holmes spoke with calm, albeit threatening, authority and this had the immediate effect of causing the author to resume his seat and calm himself.

The author took some time to gather his thoughts and he next spoke in far quieter and more placid tones than he had done previously. On Holmes's instigation, I pulled out my notebook and pencil.

'I wonder if either of you gentlemen have ever heard of Bohemian Grove?' he asked.

Holmes and I responded to this question by shrugging our shoulders and exchanging a look of nonplussed ignorance.

'There, gentlemen, is the wonder of the thing.' The author's eyes twinkled as he set about the task of illuminating us.

'The Bohemian Club was established as far back as 1872, in San Francisco, California. As the name might suggest, the club's membership was initially comprised of some of the most forward thinking and radical artists from around the globe. There were painters, sculptors, authors, and playwrights, who had all gathered together in order to exchange challenging thoughts and ideas that might inflame the established order of things, mainly within the creative arts, but not exclusively.

'Originally, the club had been established by a team of newspaper journalists. However, once the idea of a large annual gathering had been instigated, within the midst of a grove of ancient redwood trees not far from San Francisco, the "Bohemians" were commandeered by a most prominent local businessman in order that he might provide the considerable financing that was required for the purchasing and clearing of Bohemian Grove. From that very moment, the constitution and dynamics of the club changed dramatically and beyond recognition.

'Although the various artisans were still included amongst the club's membership, this was primarily so that they might provide nightly entertainments, by way of plays and lavish musicals. However, within a very short period of time the ever-expanding membership of businessmen, bankers, and politicians rose to pre-eminence and the motives behind these gatherings became rather less obvious. For two weeks, during the month of July, an enormous and lavish campsite was set out in order that these principles of industry and world leadership might gather together in a most congested form of seclusion so that they might exchange their murky and surreptitious plans.

'The view presented to any undesirable interloper would be one of festivities, celebrations, and garish rituals. However, the meetings that might have been taking place, within those luxurious walls of guarded canvas, will shape the future of the globe and its entire population.'

The author paused from his extraordinary explanation that he might bring out a decanter of the finest malt whisky that I had ever tasted. This gave Holmes and I the opportunity to light our pipes and for me to rest my aching writing hand! We exchanged no comment and the respite for my hand was to be a short one. We each took long draughts from our glasses, yet we barely had the time to savour the delights of that golden elixir before that literary prophet resumed his narrative.

'American Presidents and other heads of state are regular visitors to the Grove; however, the most preeminent and influential amongst these are the bankers. Of these there is one family in particular who stand out—'

'One moment' Holmes interposed, and leaned forward in his chair. 'You are undoubtedly a very fine teller of tales, as your published status readily attests to; however, we are still no nearer to discovering the source of those revolutionary divinations of yours. Nevertheless, we now possess a most profound knowledge of Bohemian Grove.' Our host laughed ironically at Holmes's caustic sarcasm.

'Oh Mr Holmes, I am most surprised to note that you have missed the point entirely. You see, Bohemian Grove is the source of my inspiration and predictions!' the author declared.

'Pray continue,' Holmes invited, and he crossed his thin legs in his customary languid fashion while he closed his eyes in contemplation.

I flexed my fingers once again in anticipation of another exhaustive use of my notebook. However, our host's narrative was surprisingly and mercifully close to its conclusion.

'As you must have guessed by now, I have in fact attended one of these bizarre gatherings, although not, I must add, as a full member of the Bohemians. My standing within a particular Masonic lodge, together with my reputation within the world of literature, has afforded me with the acquaintance of several members of the Bohemian Club who managed to obtain for me a statutory membership.

'I must confess that my innate curiosity had compelled me to attend, albeit against my better judgement. Naturally, I was not granted access to the more restricted and elitist areas of the facility. Nevertheless, I was able to witness one of the supposed highlights of these gatherings, a huge paganised ritual that centred on the raised stone statue of a forty-foot-high owl, and which also involved an alarming, simulated ceremony of human sacrifice!'

Holmes and I exchanged looks of great excitement at the mention of this gigantic bird, for that particular symbol had also appeared upon a communication that we had once received regarding the Bavarian Brotherhood.[13] The author appeared oblivious to our reaction, and cleared his throat before continuing.

'I had found the hedonistic and debauched atmosphere to be both contemptible and repugnant to my senses. Many of these lords of industry and commerce cavorted around the

---

[13]   From 'Sherlock Holmes and the Unholy Trinity' by P.D.G.

place in various states of undress and intoxication, and the byword was undoubtedly that of excess.

'However, I soon discovered that these orgies of perversion were merely an expression of the member's contempt for what you and I would regard as virtuous behaviour. I soon came to realise that they formed part of a façade that camouflaged the senior member's true intentions: nothing less than the establishment of a new world order fashioned from the ashes of three cataclysmic wars.

'On the one occasion when I did gain a brief access to one of these secure enclaves, I managed to ascertain the nature of the tools that they intended to have at their disposal. Fortunately, my unintentional intrusion went undetected; otherwise, I am certain that we should not be having this conversation today. It was that information that led me to the formulation of my novel.

'You see, gentlemen, my book should not be misconstrued as an indication of my collusion with these warped and dystopian plans. My intention is to present a warning to the next generation, in the hope that by establishing a fairer and more compassionate society they might yet thwart the plans of their would-be rulers.'

'I see that your reputation as a proponent of the socialist ideology is not entirely without foundation,' Holmes stated quietly, although not with the tone of condemnation that I might normally have expected from him.

Slowly Holmes began to gather up the papers and, as he rose to take his leave, he smiled when he observed the author's acceptance of his previous assertion.

'We seem to understand each other, and I apologise for having taken up so much of your valuable time.' Holmes pointed to my notebook and indicated that I too should prepare to take my leave. However, I was not quite ready yet to follow his bidding.

'You alluded to an influential family of bankers a moment ago,' I pointed out, 'although you did not go so far as to actually putting a name to them.'

'You are quite correct, Dr Watson, and for the sake of your own well-being, I have absolutely no intention of doing so. Suffice it to say that by the use of their unfathomable assets and wealth they have managed to impregnate themselves within all of the principle chancelleries of Europe. There is not a government or a politician who does not owe their position and privileges to this family, and there is not a deed or undertaking that they would not sanction or perpetrate in order that they might preserve them.

'I beseech you not to pursue this matter further, gentlemen,' The author concluded with heartfelt sincerity as he led us towards the door. However, I could perceive from his steely intensity that my friend had absolutely no intention of heeding this most dire and sincere of warnings.

CHAPTER THIRTEEN

THE BLACK MASK

At this juncture I should excuse myself to my readers for not having made mention of the name of our author and host. I assure you that this omission is not one born of discourtesy or disrespect, but more of concern for his safety; indeed, for much the same reasons that he had cited for withholding the name of the bankers from Holmes and me. The justification for our precautionary measures will one day become only too apparent.

We delayed our return to King's cab by lighting our cigarettes and indulging in a closer examination of the canal that had bordered our host's property. Although the temperature was barely hovering above the point of freezing, the cracks that were beginning to appear upon the water's icy surface were little more than merely hairline, and the reeds that threatened to choke the life from that stagnant waterway were still being bowed by the weight of the early morning frost. The silence, broken only by the sounds of our boots upon the crumbling ice sheet, was complete and most unnerving. We beat a hasty retreat back to our ride.

I had, in all honesty, half expected to find our driver asleep within his cab. After all, when we had last seen him,

King had been about to wrap himself up in a warm woollen blanket, while cradling a small flask within his frozen fingers.

To my surprise, however, the complete opposite proved to be the case. King was sitting bolt upright upon his seat and he still held the reins firmly within his grasp, in a decidedly alert and apprehensive fashion. Immediately sensing our surprise and concern, King pointed discreetly towards the rear of a vehicle, very similar to his own, that was protruding from around the corner to our left.

'They arrived within seconds of you going inside,' he replied quietly to our questioning expressions.

'Is the driver alone?' I asked.

'I would say not, Watson,' Holmes answered, casting a suspicious eye in their direction. 'In fact, judging by the distance between the arches and the wheels, I would ascertain that the carriage contains two rather substantial passengers.'

'That would be my estimate too, Mr 'Olmes,' King confirmed.

'I think that we should waste no time in discovering what their true intentions are, eh Watson?'

I nodded my wholehearted confirmation and it was decided that Holmes would make a stealthy approach to that rogue hansom, while I covered his advance from a distance with my revolver. By an unfortunate coincidence, as Holmes drew ever closer to his quarry, their horse suddenly reared up in revolt while emitting a horrendous chorus of neighs. Naturally enough, their driver was immediately alerted to Holmes's intentions and he picked up his reigns with a sharp snap, while his passengers opened fire on Holmes from the passenger seats.

I returned their fire as I retreated to and then boarded our cab, while King began to wheel the vehicle round and towards their direction. The other driver was dressed entirely in black, and the fact that he also sported a top hat caused the vehicle and its occupants to appear be all the more mysterious and sinister in appearance. King immediately gave chase as the other cab sped away, trusting in Holmes's ability to alight on to a moving vehicle. As we turned a sharp corner, Holmes leapt towards us and grabbed hold of a rail on the side of the cab, while his innate agility and lightness of foot ensured a safe collection. With much relief and a sharp intake of breath, Holmes ordered King to proceed in hot pursuit.

Initially, this was something that King was well able to execute and he did so with an exuberant relish. The long and lazy country roads afforded very little opportunity for the other cab to avoid our detection and pursuit, and the road's uneven and icy surface precluded any marked increases in their speed. On occasion, King managed to make up some ground on our quarry; however, each time that he did so our adversaries set us back by firing off repeated and malicious salvos in the direction of King's noble steed. Mercifully, each one of these went harmlessly astray.

With the welfare of his horse in mind, King now decided to maintain a more consistent distance until he was on the more familiar territory of Central London. He explained that the build of his rival's horse was better suited to speed than his, but the durability of our steed was proven and beyond question. This strange race of ours settled into a sedate and repetitive rhythm, and as I finally sank back into my seat, I realised that the early midwinter twilight had suddenly doused the surrounding countryside in a wave of shimmering gold.

The shapes of the legions of lifeless trees, now bereft of their leaves, had assumed an angry and distorted demeanour, while the birds flittered from tree to tree but found little shelter from the cold within those barren boughs. I shuddered involuntarily as a result of this observation of mine. King immediately offered me his flask and Holmes chuckled when he noticed my enthusiastic acceptance.

The golden hue suddenly transformed into a shimmering bluish shade of black and as the stars and planets re-emerged for the coming night, we also noticed a distant faint wall of light that heralded our slow return to the outskirts and the numerous gaslights of South London.

At the first sign of our imminent return to the metropolis, our quarry noticeably increased their speed. King followed suit at once, and before too long the nostrils of both horses began to produce a dense and erratic plume of steam on the out-breath. My friend, who had remained silent throughout the majority of this chase, suddenly tensed and advised me to maintain my grip upon my revolver.

'Who are these people, Holmes, and what possible reason could there be for them being here?' I asked.

'Without sufficient data it is hard to say,' said he, 'but with none at all it is impossible. However, it would appear to be fairly obvious that we have been held under a most discreet and expert surveillance, and for some considerable time. I am sure that the name of its instigator must occur to you also.'

'Gruner, of course!' I exclaimed excitedly, but Holmes did not share my enthusiasm for such an obvious conclusion. Clearly he was greatly concerned at the notion of our adversary, one so intent on revenge and retribution, being in such close proximity and possessing such intimate knowledge of our comings and goings. Holmes bit down upon his pipe stem pensively and creased his brows in deep and agonised furrows. His appearance left me feeling greatly disconcerted and I returned my attention to the ever-changing landscape that we were passing through.

To avoid the attentions of our adversaries and their revolvers, King had clearly decided to maintain an unvarying distance between the two cabs. However, as our surroundings became more urbanised, he was also aware of the need to pay attention to our enemies' every move. Potential deviations and turnings began to appear with an increasing regularity and the cab ahead cut inches from the corners of every turn.

'Blimey, Mr 'Olmes, this bloke seems to know the streets of London almost as well as I do!' King declared with undisguised admiration.

As we approached the river, I could see the soaring walls and chimney stacks of Hampton Court Palace peering majestically through the gathering gloom and mist. We crossed over from South London at Chiswick and there was no mistaking the ironically austere walls of the Fuller's brewery as we drew near to Hammersmith.

The majestic steed ahead of us tirelessly pulled its burden onward and away from us, and despite King's expertly executed attempts at wending his way through the onrushing traffic and manoeuvring our cab around the many back doubles that he knew so well, the vehicle ahead continuously forged away from us.

Finally, in a last desperate attempt at overhauling our quarry, King ducked down a wide and muddy alleyway that served the many stores that lined the adjacent street. His intention had clearly been to re-emerge at a point ahead of the rival cab. However, at the very moment of our emergence, a night-time delivery cart started down the alley towards us from the opposite direction. We were trapped! King immediately jumped down and implored the delivery driver to reverse, in terms that can only be best described as raucous and colourful. His threats and expletives, however, were to no avail and, naturally, by the time that we had managed to turn about and then retrace our steps, the other cab was nowhere to be seen.

'Damn!' Holmes exclaimed, and he remained silent and disconsolate throughout the remainder of our journey back to 221B Baker Street. As he jumped down from the cab, Holmes attempted to console King with a slap on the shoulder and a roll of bank notes into his hand.

Then, as if he had been suddenly struck by an awful realisation, Holmes asked the stalwart driver to wait while he sprinted away up the stairs, leaving King as nonplussed as I had been. My friend returned a moment later and hurriedly thrust an envelope into the cabby's hand.

'Please deliver this into the hands of Inspector Lestrade at Scotland Yard, with as much speed as your poor old animal can still muster,' Holmes requested sympathetically. King doffed his cap with a steely determination and was gone.

'Watson,' Holmes explained in answer to my look of perplexity, 'I greatly fear for the life of our friend in Woking, and I have implored Lestrade to visit him at once and to arrange for his security until such time as he can vacate his current premises.'

'Do you honestly expect a man of such standing to pack up and move home, without a single word of explanation? After all, you cannot be certain that his life is really under threat,' I queried.

'I do not expect it, Watson, I demand it! Gruner and his people have gone to great lengths in ascertaining the route that our investigation has taken and I can assure you that if they have even an inkling of the information that our friend possesses, his life will not be worth a moment's purchase! Besides, based upon the chaotic storage of his books and papers and the absence of any articles of a personal nature being on display, I would say that his is only a temporary accommodation,' Holmes concluded.

'Now that you come to mention it, there was not one family picture or portrait anywhere to be seen . . .'

At that moment our landlady suddenly appeared on the front step, waving at us in a state of great agitation. We ran towards her at once and followed her dutifully up the stairs to our rooms. I helped her into one of our chairs and then poured her a small glass of calming brandy. This she steadfastly refused and so I ended up draining the glass myself.

'Pray compose yourself, Mrs Hudson,' Holmes requested with surprising tenderness, 'and explain to me the events that have troubled you so.'

'Oh, Mr Holmes,' she began, while catching her breath and gathering her thoughts. 'This awful couple arrived shortly after you and Dr Watson had departed on your jaunt and demanded that they be allowed to await your return in your chambers, as their business with you was of a most urgent nature. Under normal circumstances I would not have allowed such a thing, but I knew that you were working on one of your cases and I had no idea how important they might have been to your investigation.'

'You did the right thing, Mrs Hudson,' I assured the poor woman with a smile.

Despite his best efforts, Holmes could not disguise his impatience. He crooked his finger by way of an invitation for our beleaguered landlady to continue.

'Mrs Hudson, I need you describe to me, in as much detail as you can recall, the appearance of this awful couple of yours.'

'It should not be so hard for me to remember such a pair, but not so easy for me to put it into words.' She looked up at my friend helplessly.

'In that case, let me see if I can help you,' Holmes suggested with an enigmatic smile.

Our landlady sat back in her chair with a faintly sceptical look on her pale face, while Holmes slowly lit a cigarette.

'Unless I am very much mistaken, Mrs Hudson, I would say that the woman was in her mid- to late twenties, strikingly tall and elegant, and that she was dressed from head to toe in black, thereby accentuating her uncommonly blonde head of very long hair . . .'

Mrs Hudson's expression transformed from the cynical to the awestruck and as Holmes continued to speak, her eyes and mouth progressively widened.

'There is certainly something uncanny in all of this,' said she, looking to me for reassurance. I merely shrugged resignedly; after all, this was a scenario that I had been witness to on a myriad of other occasions.

'Her male consort,' Holmes continued, 'was of a far less remarkable appearance, although no less memorable despite his visual anonymity. He was of a similar height to his companion, with a robust build and bearing. However, he would have had a tendency to conceal his face, probably by way of wearing his muffler and collar high and his hat low. I would also not be in the least bit surprised if he had feigned a cough and cold, thereby giving him the excuse to cover his face at every opportunity. Undoubtedly, they both spoke with pronounced Germanic accents.' Holmes smiled with satisfaction when he observed the look of stupefaction upon our landlady's face.

I, on the other hand, had been left in little doubt that our visitors had been none other than Baron Gruner and his daughter.

'Well, I must say, Mr Holmes, if I had not known any better, I would say that you had concealed yourself in this room during their visit,' Mrs Hudson exclaimed.

'Assuming that I did nothing of the sort, could you explain why their behaviour unsettled you so?' Holmes asked.

'Their manner was most intimidating, Mr Holmes, and I felt strangely compelled to show them to your rooms despite my better judgement. The strange thing was that although they seemed to be quite content to wait for your return, and they both settled into their chairs as if they were expecting a long stay, within a few minutes of my leaving them there, they both upped and left and scuttled down the stairs without so much as a by your leave!'

'That is odd,' I agreed. 'Clearly they had no intention of confronting us, for they had previously gone to such great lengths in ascertaining and confirming our absence. Surely they had not expected us to leave those cursed papers lying around?'

Holmes silenced me with an impatient wave of his hand, then he pressed his lips with his right forefinger while he considered all of the potential options. By now, Mrs Hudson felt steady enough to take her leave, and as she clearly had nothing further to contribute, Holmes dismissed her with an urgent request for a strong cup of black coffee.

Holmes moved across to the window, but from the corner of his eyes he caught sight of an object that had not been present on the dining table prior to our departure. For there, lying in an untidy bundle, lay a black silk mask of the sort that Baron Gruner had been wont to wear.

'Watson, I have erred like an abject fool!' He spat these words out with a rasping hiss of self-disgust.

'Oh, surely not, Holmes.' My plaintive and futile attempt at words of consolation did little towards placating my friend's ire.

'It is gone, Watson, and like a dullard I have allowed it to fall into the hands of our enemies!' Holmes snatched up the black mask and then hurled it petulantly into the heart of the roaring fire. Within seconds every fibre had been devoured by the flames. Holmes observed this process with wide and frenzied eyes.

'You see, Watson, how the flames symbolically rent asunder any notions of success that we might have previously been harbouring?' Holmes pointed towards the grate as if I had previously been oblivious of its existence.

'The envelope, Watson, the very envelope that had brought these papers to our door, is now in their possession,' Holmes explained excitedly in answer to my look of confusion as he allowed the papers to fall to the floor at his feet.

'It is only an envelope, old fellow; surely no serious harm can come from that?' I reasoned.

'It is also an envelope that bares the return to sender's address on the back!' Holmes exclaimed, as much out of exasperation as of despair.

It did not take me long to appreciate the cause of Holmes's emotional outburst, and the threat now posed to his brother Mycroft was immediately clear.

'We must wire him at once!' Holmes declared, and the ferocity of his summons to Mrs Hudson caused our long-suffering landlady to stumble through our doorway, thereby spilling the majority of Holmes's freshly made coffee. Holmes immediately dismissed the remainder of his drink and despatched the poor woman with his scrawled-out message.

I immediately dived into my trusty Bradshaw's, but then added further to my friend's angst, for it revealed that there were to be no further trains until the following lunchtime. Holmes immediately secured the papers in his desk drawer and I could see that he had been more than a little tempted to remove his Moroccan leather case at the same time. This case, of course, contained his hypodermic syringe, but to his credit, after a long and wistful glance at this enticing object, he relocked the desk and tossed the key over to me for safekeeping.

Instead, Holmes lit and smoked a succession of cigarettes before realising that his state of anxiety had become nothing more than a futile exercise. Shortly afterwards, his mood had been tempered somewhat by a message received from Inspector Lestrade. He had acted upon Holmes's suggestion and assured us that our author friend's home was to receive a far closer surveillance from the Woking constabulary than had been the norm. Furthermore, he had received assurances from its occupant that plans for vacating his temporary home were to be instigated with immediate effect.

'Those long and insidious fingers seem able to penetrate into the very heart of everything that we hold dear, eh Watson?' Holmes suggested quietly as he slumped into his chair, as if his nervous tension had drained every ounce of energy that he possessed. On the other hand, I supposed, perhaps the monumental size of the task that now lay ahead of him was weighing down upon him more heavily than any that he had yet encountered. Even with my own limited understanding of what that might have entailed, I was not in the least bit surprised at his uncharacteristic reaction.

In an attempt at arresting my friend's descent into one of his brown moods, I decided to venture a discussion upon the subject of that mysterious and influential banking house that the author had made brief mention of, by way of the gravest of warnings. Mycroft had made a brief mention of such a possibility in his letter and Holmes had already reached a conclusion as to the identity of this institution.

'They are untouchable, Watson,' he stated simply, although with much gravity in his tone.

'Surely no one is beyond the law?' I ventured, but half-heartedly.

'That status is not a hard one to achieve if one happens to *be* the law. The family in question is large enough for them to have been able to connect themselves to every principle dynasty in Europe; from the Balkans to the Atlantic, you will find one of their clan. Watson, they are so wealthy and influential that the acquisition of currency is now no longer their goal. The size of their fortune is inconsequential when you compare it to their quest and lust for power.

'So successful have they been, that now barely a single decision made on foreign affairs, by any government you might care to mention, including our own, is made without the authority or suggestion of these financial potentates. Obviously, because of the very nature of his unique and surreptitious position in government, my brother is probably the only person, outside of that select and manipulative circle, who has even an inkling of their dark and far-reaching designs.

'The importance that he attaches to their plans can best be gauged by the fact that he, of all people, could be galvanised into pursuing a plan of action that removed him from his regular and comfortable daily regime. No, Watson, our best course of action would be to leave them to their own devices and concentrate our efforts on combating those who operate under their instructions. After all, a queen bee would be of very little use without her army of drones.' Holmes concluded this longer than anticipated discourse in a voice that was so faint that it was almost as if he had been talking to himself throughout.

When I did finally respond, he received my words with a jolt of surprise, so unaware of my presence had he been.

'Once again we have come full circle and arrived yet again at the threat posed by Baron Gruner and the Bavarian Brotherhood,' I said.

However, my friend was not to be drawn into any further discussion upon the subject and he sank back once more into his velvet-lined armchair with a long sigh. Evidently his thoughts were now fully focused upon the potential events that might, even now, be unfolding in the Highlands of Scotland.

Sherlock Holmes spent the remainder of that night within the confines of his chair, and his despondent outlook had been so intense that he had even refrained from his usual intake of tobacco, due, no doubt, to the effort that it might have entailed. His face had been contorted by a morass of deep lines and his eyes were held tightly shut, but not as a result of sleep.

I left him to his silent vigil and I made my way upstairs in a state of anxious despair. After a restless night, I rose early the following morning to find my friend's position had remained unchanged. He was unmoved by my greetings and did not utter a single word until the insipid winter sunlight slowly rose above the line of our windowsill.

At once he became galvanised by the thought of the hour and that our journey to Scotland was imminent. He even joined me at the dining table when Mrs Hudson brought up our breakfast tray, and although he did not partake of any of the food on offer, he drank two large cups of coffee with his cigarettes.

Once I had confirmed the train times to him, from my Bradshaw's, he made off to his room and prepared for the long journey that lay ahead.

Then the wire arrived . . .

CHAPTER FOURTEEN

BEREAVEMENT

The wire in question changed everything. It had arrived just moments before Dave 'Gunner' King had pulled up outside, ready to whisk us off to the station.

Holmes, who had been standing eagerly by the door with his coat on and with his small overnight bag in hand, had not been expecting a reply to his earlier message, and therefore tore the wire open with not a little curiosity. The effect that its contents had upon my friend was both staggering and disconcerting to any interested and educated observer.

He let the flimsy piece of paper fall forlornly to the floor and his bag dropped disinterestedly from his grasp. His eyes, which had previously gleamed with the anticipation of fresh adventure, suddenly faded.

His countenance became ashen and desolate, and his eyes glazed over with every indication of the kind of grief that I had never supposed my friend to be capable of. Even his posture suddenly deteriorated and his normally upright back sank as his shoulders dropped. Such a transformation had been shocking to behold and my instinctive reaction was to rush forward in an attempt at consoling my friend.

He had other ideas, however, and he demanded the key to his desk drawer by stretching out his hand and jerking his head towards the home of his dreaded box. Even though I had been, as yet, ignorant of the wire's content, I would have been a poor friend indeed had I not realised the futility and insensitivity of refusing my friend's demands. As he shuffled off to his room, clasping the box to him with a great but misguided reverence, he grunted his acquiescence to my reading of that traumatic message.

As I began to read, the first few lines caused me to seek the reassuring comfort of my chair and a rather substantial glass of port. As one would have expected from a firm of solicitors, the grammar was unnecessarily verbose and long-winded. However, its contents shook me to the core and I could only imagine the internal turmoil that Holmes was now undoubtedly enduring.

Starling, Williamson and Starling were a long-established family firm who had hailed from Inverness. In stark and indifferent terms, they had written to inform my friend of the violent and tragic death of his brother Mycroft Holmes!

I pushed the offending message away from me while I drank long and hard from my glass, and several minutes would pass before I felt able to resume reading. There were no details as to the actual cause of Mycroft's death, although my own instincts obviously pointed decisively towards Gruner or his confederates. Ignoring any attempts at words of condolence, the solicitors merely informed Holmes of the appointed date and time of Mycroft's funeral, and the exact location and the directions to his final resting place, all of which Mycroft seemed to have orchestrated while he was living.

Furthermore, Holmes had been invited to a reading of Mycroft's Last Will and Testament at the old drover's lodge, which had served as his Scottish place of residence. Both the cemetery and the lodge were in Upper Linnie, close to Drumnadrochit, and neither were easily accessible. The date had been set for the following Tuesday, the twenty-eighth of

December, and so I raced down the stairs to apologetically dismiss 'Gunner' King without a moment's further delay.

We certainly had time enough in which to plan our forthcoming journey, and so I turned my attention towards my friend and his bedroom door. Upon entering the room, Holmes had turned the lock with resounding determination, just so that I should know that he had no intention of resurfacing at any time in the immediate future.

I placed my ear to his door, but I could detect nothing more than an eerie and ominous silence. I gave the door a gentle rap.

'Are you all right old fellow?' I called out.

His only response had been a deep and noncommittal grunt, and so I decided to plan ahead and began to study the solicitor's instructions with my Bradshaw's guide in hand. Even if we were to use the Special Scotch Express, the journey from King's Cross to Edinburgh could not be completed in less than eight and a half hours! Obviously, that would require us to stay overnight in Edinburgh before undertaking the further three-and-a-half-hour journey to Inverness.

The thought of the remainder of our journey was beginning to make my head spin, for I knew full well that there was no train from Inverness to Drumnadrochit. I allowed the book and papers to fall to the floor and, after making one final attempt at communicating with my friend, I retired for the night.

I had been disappointed, but not altogether surprised, to discover that Holmes had absolutely no intention of leaving his room when I came downstairs the following morning. My attempts at enticing him out for some breakfast were met with a familiar silence and Mrs Hudson removed his breakfast things with a disconsolate shrug and a shaking of her head.

'I have warned him many times that he will soon fade away if he does not take some food!' she exclaimed loudly, so that Holmes might overhear her advice.

'Well, he has received a most distressing piece of news,' I informed her in defence of my friend, but it did nothing to negate her disappointment or concern.

My friend's behaviour had left me at a loss. My concern as a physician was more than matched by my personal anxieties. Therefore, by that afternoon, when it was obvious to me that Holmes had no intention of relenting, I began thumping his bedroom door with all of my might.

'Holmes, unless you unlock that door right now, I shall have no alternative other than to summon the authorities that they might break it down!' I called angrily.

I listened carefully and patiently for a moment or two before I realised, with some relief, that he was slowly making his way towards the door.

'You shall have no need of that,' he whispered hoarsely, and finally I could hear the key slowly being turned.

The evil substance that he had nurtured in that box had drained every ounce of strength and fortitude from him, and he almost fell into my arms as he staggered from his room, so emaciated had he become. His appearance shook me to the core. His bloodshot eyes had sunk back into their blackened sockets and his sheet-white features had become a morbid caricature of his former self.

'Of what use are you now to your late brother and his noble cause?' I asked harshly.

Christmas Day had come and gone without even a moment's acknowledgement within our rooms, and I began to wonder if Holmes would even be capable of making our proposed trip in two days' time.

Holmes accepted my rebuke by raising his hand in surrender and he even managed a small smile as he realised the true extent of my loyalty and friendship.

'I presume that you have put our travel arrangements into place?' he whispered.

'Indeed I have, but as a man of medicine, as well as your comrade, I would strongly advise you against attempting to fulfil them. For heaven's sake, Holmes, we have to travel in two days' time and just look at you!'

By now Holmes had reached his chair and as he eased himself down, he pulled a cigarette and a light from his dressing-gown pocket. His shaking hand was incapable of putting flame to paper so I had to assist him, although with great reluctance.

As Holmes sat there, drawing pleasurably upon the smoke, I called down to Mrs Hudson for a tray of food and a large pot of coffee. Initially, Holmes objected to my suggestion, but the look of reprimand upon our landlady's face and the possibility that he might be incapable of attending his own brother's funeral, forced him into submission.

He found the consumption of the food to be a most arduous task, although the coffee did much to re-energise him, and it restored a little of his colour. Mrs Hudson had stood over him until each and every morsel had been consumed and it was only once she had removed the tray, with triumphal satisfaction, and then marched from the room, that Holmes had felt able to explain and excuse his shameful behaviour. I attempted to make this all the easier for him by acknowledging the fact that the loss of a brother would have been enough to have traumatised any man.

Holmes shook his head gravely.

'No, Watson, not to a man of logic. There are possibilities in life, probabilities and proven certainties, but there is only one ultimate truth. One day each one of us will die. The only imponderables are the means, cause, and timing of our deaths, but our passing is inevitable nevertheless. A logician knows this with certainty, accepts it, and is, therefore, better prepared for it when that time finally arrives. Why then should the death of another be any more of a cause of distress than that of one's self?'

'Oh, come along Holmes, you do not mean to tell me that you have not been mourning the death of your brother for these past few days? The last time that I saw you with that damnable box was on the occasion when we were informed of the sudden and tragic death of our old ally Shenouda.'[14]

By now Holmes was alert enough to recognise my consternation at his apparent lack of compassionate feeling.

'Watson, you should not judge me too harshly you know. The untimely deaths of Shenouda and Mycroft have both saddened me greatly. However, the sense of guilt that I felt upon hearing of their passing far outweighed any sensation of loss that I might otherwise have experienced.' Holmes then turned sharply away from me, as if he had been concerned that his countenance might have betrayed his true feelings.

'Do you mean to say that you feel responsible for both of their deaths?' I asked, aghast at the thought of my friend labouring under such a weighty sense of remorse.

'Yes, Watson, certainly I do!' he replied emphatically. 'Do not forget that had we not accepted Shenouda's kindly offer of protection from his sentinel, the stalwart Ahkom, Shenouda should not have been struck down, in so cowardly a fashion, by our enemies. However, even that profound error of judgement pales into insignificance when compared to my flagrant disregard of my brother's safety . . .'

'Surely you cannot blame yourself for that?' I asked in astonishment.

Holmes suddenly stood up and moved over to the window. He pushed the drape to one side and peered cautiously out upon his beloved Baker Street.

'I should not be a bit surprised if we were to see some snow today, Watson,' he remarked casually, although I had been in no doubt that he had merely been distracting himself from the cause of his abasement.

When he turned towards me once more, there was an intensity in his troubled eyes such as I had never seen before.

'My own brother has paid the ultimate price for my calamitous stupidity. The envelope, Watson, with the

---

[14] From 'Sherlock Holmes and the Unholy Trinity' by P.D.G.

sender's address clearly emblazoned across its reverse. Had I not carelessly left it laying there for all to see, they would not even have been able to locate him, much less bring about his untimely death. Despite all of his precautions and meticulous planning, Mycroft has been undone by the stupid neglect of his brother! However, if I am to avenge his death, the time for lament and guilt must end now!' he declared with a rejuvenated resolve. 'Thank you, Watson.'

He slapped me upon the shoulder as he headed towards his bedroom to set about his toilet.

* * *

Mrs Hudson and I spent the next two days in the process of rebuilding the health and strength of Sherlock Holmes. His determination to purge himself of the poisons, both materially and emotionally, began with the destruction of his leather Moroccan case and, more pertinently, of its contents. Not once did he refuse any of Mrs Hudson's suggestions for food and drink, and he had slept for longer and more continuous periods of time than I had ever known him to.

By the morning of the twenty-seventh, the man standing by the front door with his overnight bag in hand had been transformed back into the Sherlock Holmes whom I had known so well. His eyes shone with a steely glitter and his rigid jawline told me that he was now ready for any of the challenges that still lay ahead, and he even broke into an encouraging smile upon observing the look of apprehension that I had failed to disguise.

Dave 'Gunner' King whisked us off to King's Cross station and before long we found ourselves aboard the Special Scotch Express bound for Edinburgh. Despite his remarkable and dramatic recovery, Holmes still refused to be drawn into any form of conversation, much less upon the subject of the matter in hand, and as the hours and the miles sped by, I was left amazed by his stoic refusal to abandon his meditational posture and the peace of mind that this practice apparently bestowed upon him.

We had the carriage to ourselves, and yet, not for the first time, I found that I was left to my own devices. Consequently, I decided to explore the recently installed corridors and I even ventured to sample the most limited cuisine being plied by the buffet car. Finally, I settled into my seat and soon became enthralled by the rapidly changing landscapes.

It seemed that the further north that we travelled, the more prevalent became the icy conditions. I was reminded of my trek through Central Europe, where I had become equally captivated by the undulating hills and mountains, and the harshness of their backdrop of snow. Once we had passed through the Staffordshire Potteries and the Black Country, my thoughts began to turn more and more towards Mycroft's funeral and the threat that was still being posed by Baron Gruner. As a matter of fact, the tragic demise of Mycroft Holmes had actually enhanced the dark shadow that Gruner still cast over us.

He must have been certain by now that the Brotherhood's all-important papers were still in our possession. However, we could not be sure if our departure had been observed, nor even if Gruner was still in Scotland and awaiting our arrival with a deadly intent. He had already proven the extent of his lethal determination, and in the most tragic way imaginable. Consequently, I became determined to maintain an alert and suspicious vigilance throughout the remainder of our journey.

Holmes finally broke away from his silent contemplation when we pulled into the station at York. In the days before the buffet car had been installed, York had served as the only potential venue for lunch available to a hungry passenger. Although this was no longer the case, the truncated fifteen-minute interlude provided us with the opportunity to stretch our legs and light up a pipe or two.

My friend had taken full advantage of both opportunities, and he had even purchased a cold meat sandwich from a convenient vendor on the platform. Now suitably refreshed and revitalised, Holmes and I returned to our carriage and, more significantly, with Holmes more conducive to the idea of discussion and conversation.

Holmes unbuttoned his coat and threw down his hat and muffler on to the seat next to him in a most dramatic fashion. He rubbed his hands together repeatedly and stared at me with a smile, as if in anticipation of a pent-up barrage of questions. In that he had been mistaken, for I merely requested that he allay my anxious anticipation by giving voice to any thoughts that he might have had upon the conclusion to this matter.

He lit a cigarette and then stared into my eyes for what had seemed to have been an interminable length of time, as if he had been trying to gauge the effect that his words might have had upon me. Apparently, he had been left satisfied by his conclusions.

'What you have asked of me is no easy task, Watson, especially as my perspective may have become somewhat compromised by the lamentable news about my brother. Nevertheless, it now occurs to me that it would be unjust of me to expect you to join me upon the final phase of our crusade without you having an insight into the potential outcome and repercussions, albeit from my own limited perspective.

'Undoubtedly there would be those, of a certain philosophical viewpoint, who would regard the Brotherhood's vision of the future in a positive light. After all, the successful completion of their scheme would result in a stability and worldwide peace that, hitherto, would have been deemed as impossible to even conceive.

'Nevertheless, those potential benefits must be weighed against the inevitable sacrifices and costs that would undoubtedly have to be levied in order to achieve such a noble vision.' There was a bitter sarcasm in Holmes's tone that alerted me to his disgust at such a notion.

'This "utopian" society can only be achieved through the eradication of basic human rights, freedom, and democracy, and then culminating in a cataclysmic loss of life! If you were to imagine the most dictatorial autocracy that has ever existed in human history — the Roman Empire immediately springs to mind — and then visualise their heartless and relentless achievements on a global scale, then you would have just a glimpse of the form of enslavement that they have in mind for us. Would you consider this to be a price worth paying for the self-serving schemes of a select and privileged few?'

'I most certainly would not!' I answered emphatically.

Holmes slapped his thigh triumphantly.

'I certainly know, my Watson,' he beamed.

'Of course, from a more personal and professional perspective, their success would also bring to an end the many centuries that have been spent in mankind's pursuit of justice for the common man. As you know, this has been the very bedrock of all that my humble practise and career have stood for, and all that I have striven to achieve.' Holmes's impassioned statement had clearly left him emotionally exhausted and he sank back into his seat with a deep sigh.

'In all honesty, Holmes, do you think that we two alone can bring about the destruction of the Brotherhood and their plans?' I asked, more out of hope than expectation. I was left greatly deflated by Holmes's solemn shake of his head and by his inevitable reply.

'No, Watson, I do not; but pray consider the facts. Under a series of different names and guises, the organisation that we are aiming to obstruct has in all probability been in existence for many centuries, perhaps as far back as the Roman Empire itself. One could even argue the case that the Empire has never really fallen, despite Gibbon's assertions to the contrary.

'Throughout that time, their contemptuous and grandiose plans have been evolving and propagating, and then finally culminating in those papers that we have removed from the desk of Baron Gruner. Can you really countenance the notion that every consideration for the success of their schemes has not been meticulously calculated, and that two isolated individuals can do anything to thwart them?' Holmes asked.

'I suppose not,' I admitted grudgingly.

Holmes eyed my despondency with surprising sympathy.

'You should not despair, Watson, for although we may not be able to completely thwart them in their schemes, we do have the advantage of being the only men alive that are aware of them. We have come a long way since our discovery of their existence and, as we have proven on more than one occasion, they are not entirely invulnerable.'

Having imparted to me this small glimmer of hope, my friend sank back again into his seat and closed his eyes. He would not open them again until we had finally pulled into Waverley station in Edinburgh.

My Bradshaw's guide had shown that there would not be a connecting train to Inverness until the following morning, so Holmes and I had arranged rooms for ourselves at the hotel, which bore the name of the station and lay in close proximity to the terminus. This fine establishment afforded us an excellent meal and some warm comfort prior to the somewhat harsher conditions that we anticipated on the following day.

As we approached the hotel, I was taken aback by the imposing walls and towers of the castle that loomed majestically above the city. Fashioned from the light grey local sandstone that seemed to constitute the majority of the surrounding buildings, at times it was barely distinguishable through the dark swirling mists of similar hue.

I was resolved to a post-dinner constitutional along Princes Street, that I might appreciate the city's magnificence all the more. However, the harsh elements soon forced me to a hasty retreat and I had barely finished my cigar before I sought the refuge of our hotel once more. Holmes appeared to be maliciously amused by my plight as he luxuriated in the warmth of the large and embracing fireplace.

It had been as well that we had arranged for an early breakfast, for our train's early departure had proved to be more than a little punctual, and we had barely climbed aboard before the train had lurched into its uneven motion. The one-hundred-and-thirteen-mile journey, on the Highland Railway to Inverness, lasted a laborious three-and-a-half hours and upon our eventual arrival we realised that we needed to secure the services of a horse and trap without delay, if we were not to be late for Mycroft's funeral!

In this we proved to be successful and we were soon negotiating the final sixteen miles of our odyssey. Occasionally, our tiny vehicle skirted the very shores of Loch Ness itself, although at the time it had been partially shrouded in the all-pervading mist. Nevertheless, there had been no escaping its timeless, mystical allure and I resolved to pay this vast lake another visit, although under hopefully less frenetic circumstances.

The undulating nature of the road resulted in a reduction in speed that Holmes had found to be both irritating and fretful. He constantly pulled out his timepiece and on each occasion that the cart had been slowed down by a sharp rise or by a sudden bend in the road, my friend had snapped his watch cover shut and ground his teeth audibly. I checked the letter from Starling, Williamson and Starling and then my own timepiece before appreciating how justified had been my friend's anxiety.

Frustratingly, our progress had been further hampered by the uneven nature of the trail and, at times, the various rocks and small boulders that festooned the track were positively treacherous. So much so, in fact, that on more than one occasion we were actually forced to pull up and then climb down in order to remove them from our path.

As we finally reached the southernmost extremities of the loch, we were greeted by an alteration in the weather that was as appreciated as it had been extreme. A strong offshore breeze had transformed the sheet of fog into a column of white and wispy clouds that had soon been dissipated into the horizon. This sudden change in conditions had brought about a dual advantageous effect upon our journey.

Our driver had now been able to proceed with a good deal more confidence than he had previously, which had naturally led to a marked increase in the speed of our progress. Furthermore, our improved visibility had also revealed to us the small hamlet of Upper Linnie, wherein we knew could be found the Scottish abode of the late Mycroft Holmes, namely the stately old drover's lodge.

Holmes soon came to the same realisation and he immediately replaced his timepiece with his tobacco pouch as it dawned on him that he was about to attend the funeral of his beloved elder brother.

'Holmes, do you anticipate a large attendance at the graveside?' I asked once the small, tree-lined cemetery finally came into view from behind one of the foothills of Glen Urquhart.

My friend could barely suppress his amusement at what I had considered to be quite a reasonable question.

'No, Watson, I certainly do not. Apart from us, there should be no one there apart from one or two servants, the gravediggers, a lawyer or two, and potentially Miss Vukovic. Surprisingly, you seem to forget that my brother had been one of the founding members of the Diogenes Club, an establishment that, without a doubt, was comprised of the most misanthropic membership that one could possibly imagine! No, Watson, you can be assured that the gathering shall be a small one.'

As we drew ever closer, it soon became apparent that, for once, my friend's reasoning could not have been further from the truth. Once the last remnants of the flimsy clouds had beaten their retreat, a sparkling array of winter sunshine revealed our surroundings in all of their natural splendour. Even the small graveyard assumed an unexpectedly attractive allure and it appeared to have been a lot more densely populated than my friend had anticipated!

Although there had clearly been no fresh snow fall for many a day, the intensity of the cold had rendered the ground snow with a texture that bore a closer resemblance to dry balls of ice. As we climbed down from the cart, a strong gust of mountain air whisked piles of these balls into a whirlpool of flying ice, which peppered our faces in a series of painful punctures. We dismissed our driver with a well-earned gratuity, as the lawyers had promised us a carriage to Mycroft's lodge at the conclusion of the service.

The cemetery had no chapel of its own; therefore, the local clergyman had decided to conduct the service by the graveside. It had been a universally unpopular decision, given the prevalent Arctic conditions, and I concluded that there had been many a silent and private prayer offered up that day, in the hope that the service be a brief one!

I cast a concerned glance towards my friend and saw at once that the weather had been the least of his concerns. Even a man such as he, one who deliberately eschewed emotion in favour of reason, logic, and exact knowledge, could not have failed to have been moved at the sight of his brother's coffin being borne towards us. Even so, as the small ceremonial group drew ever closer to us, I saw Holmes's demeanour change suddenly and inexplicably, and instead he turned his attention pointedly towards the identities of the unexpectedly large gathering.

CHAPTER FIFTEEN

ILLUMINATION

The six pall-bearers had certainly been labouring under the weight of so large a coffin, and this had become most apparent when they had endeavoured to slide it out from the horse-drawn hearse. Mercifully for them, the distance between the hearse and the graveside had been a relatively short one, otherwise their insecure footing, created by the ground's icy surface, might have climaxed in a calamitous result.

As Holmes and I approached the open grave, a tall, trimly built man, of a most austere demeanour, stepped out from the crowd to greet us with an outstretched hand. This gentleman, as it transpired, was Mr Daniel Starling, the senior partner at Mycroft's chosen firm of solicitors. He had clearly been detrimentally affected by the severe conditions, because the hand that he had offered shook most violently and his caught breath had rendered his offer of condolence as barely audible.

'Mr Starling,' offered Holmes, 'I congratulate you upon the arrangements, made under so singularly extreme a set of conditions.'

'I assure you, Mr Holmes, that we merely followed your brother's most explicit instructions as best we could.' Starling bowed as he retreated into the relative comfort of the centre of the crowd.

As the only mourner, Holmes cut a most isolated figure as he stood to attention by the side of his brother's grave, his tall, gaunt figure made even gaunter and taller by his long travelling cloak and close-fitting cloth cap. Consequently, although it was not strictly the correct protocol for me to have done so, I felt duty bound to assume a position by his side.

As the service progressed, I used the vantage point to observe the remainder of the congregation.

It goes without saying that Miss Vukovic had been the most conspicuous member of that assembly. This had been partially due to her striking and most singular appearance, and her apparent indifference to the cold, but primarily because she had been the only woman in attendance.

Then, as I expanded my field of observation, I began to identify a small group of Mycroft's former colleagues at the Diogenes Club, two or three of Mycroft's subordinates at his offices in Whitehall, and I was surprised to see that even his valet, from his Pall Mall lodgings, had somehow made his way to this remote Highlands hamlet.

However, the most striking aspect of my reconnaissance had not been any of these, or the presence of a few of the high-ranking politicians who had, at some time or another, come within the sphere of Mycroft's governmental influence. Most notable of all had been the presence of so many similarly attired gentlemen of whose identity I had no notion whatsoever.

I had glanced across at my friend, and I could see that he had been similarly fascinated by this aspect of the arcane congregation. Holmes smiled at me enigmatically and at once my mind went back to the funeral of his former associate, Langdale Pike.[15] The mourners that had been present that day at the Brompton cemetery had also been most notable

---

[15]   From 'The Four-Handed Game' by P.D.G. and 'The Adventure of the Final Problem' by Sir A.C.D.

by virtue of their apparent anonymity, and had it not been for the avaricious and diligent undertaker, their significant identities would have remained unknown to us to this day.

I knew at once that the congregants in question had not been there to mourn the passing of Mycroft Holmes, but more to confirm it! Who amongst them might still have had a significant role to play in the drama that was still to unfold?

My benign reverie was suddenly brought to an involuntary conclusion by the sight of Mycroft's coffin being slowly lowered into the frozen, gaping chasm that had been fashioned for his final place of rest. In an instant the congregation, that a moment before had been huddled together in a pathetic and comforting group, had been violently dispersed by an intense gust of chill wind that had been both cruel and unrelenting.

The piles of icy globules had been suddenly whipped up into an erratic frenzy and they had spun to such a height that it seemed as if they had become a part of a fresh fall of snow. These diaphanous white columns flitted back and forth from gravestone to gravestone and to an undisciplined and imaginative mind, might have resembled the restless and tortured spirits of the dead.

I was certain that no such thoughts would have occurred to my pragmatic friend, and that he had been more concerned by the fact that this sudden exodus would ensure the continued anonymity of the unknown mourners. He grunted as they hurriedly returned to their various vehicles, and after a brief and quiet moment of reflection by the graveside, Holmes turned his reluctant attention towards the carriage that awaited our return.

The two magnificent bays bowed their heads in deference to the elements and seemed almost grateful when we finally climbed aboard and gave our instructions to the driver. He, in turn, was huddled beneath a thick greatcoat, a huge muffler and a ridiculously tall, black hat that had been pulled down as far as it would go. The valet and Miss Vukovic had already taken their seats, and our small mournful group sat in silence as our carriage carefully picked its way through the rough and slowly rising terrain.

Miss Vukovic extended her elegant, leather-clad hand and offered her condolences to my friend in a hushed and surprisingly heartfelt tone. Holmes, however, appeared to have been preoccupied and I wondered if his observations had revealed something that my own had not. He quelled any notion of my questions by shaking his head and pursing his lips with his finger.

'It is most gracious of you, Miss Vukovic, to pay such homage to my brother,' said he, clearly in an attempt at further diverting my curiosity.

'Mr Holmes has always been most kind and generous towards me, and I owe him much,' the young assassin responded quietly with a sad smile, and she turned her attention towards the snow clouds that were slowly gathering to the north.

Mercifully, we started up the drive towards Mycroft's lodge before they began to discard their treacherous load, and it was immediately decided that both the lawyer, who was in a small carriage behind ours, and our own driver would be put up overnight in the event of the likely meteorological assault.

Ahead of us the elegant, double-fronted building came into view and, although it was somewhat smaller than I had imagined it would be, I had been impressed by the seclusion that had been created by its frame of densely grouped Scots pine trees. Rather uniquely, perhaps, because of its original intended use, the lodge boasted two identical entrances that divided the building into two wings. There was an adjacent barn, towards which the carriages had been hastily led by an eager young stable boy.

The young servant's urgency was well founded, for the anticipated blizzard began but a few moments after he had settled the horses into their warm, hay-lined shelter. Mycroft's valet set about the task of reinvigorating the fire, while the other servant went outside to ensure that everything was safely secured.

By the time that he had returned, to secure the front door and the shutters, we four were already settled in front of the fire and ready for Mr Starling to begin the reading of the will. Holmes halted him before he had even begun, and demanded to know the whereabouts of our driver.

'Perhaps he has decided to stay with his horse?' I ventured.

'No, no, no,' Holmes tutted, clearly perplexed by this strange turn of events.

'We would surely have noticed him either come in or go upstairs?' Starling suggested.

It was decided that Holmes and I would search the rooms upstairs while the valet and Miss Vukovic ventured outside to check the barn. Our search on the upper floor proved to be a fruitless one and Holmes's anxiety increased when the other search party had failed to return from the barn within an appropriate length of time. I moved determinedly towards the door, but my friend held me back temporarily.

'Watson, I would advise you to you take every precaution.' He said gravely, and I immediately removed my revolver from my coat pocket, only too well aware of his meaning.

I stood by the open door and immediately observed how quickly the severity of the storm had filled in and smoothed over every footprint. I had taken only a step or two before I had been confronted by the sight of Miss Vukovic staggering through the obscurity of the snowstorm towards me with the powerful arm of the driver wrapped tightly around her slender neck. In his other hand, the driver held a revolver, which pressed tightly against the young lady's temple!

Only then did I realise that the man gesturing for me to return to the lodge with aggressive urgency had also been wearing a black silk mask across his face!

I discreetly slid my gun back into its pocket and then staggered uncertainly back into the building with the driver, who I now knew to be none other than Baron Gruner, in close attendance. His mask creased up as the face beneath it broke into a malicious smile, and as we all passed through the door, Gruner slammed it fiercely behind him. I joined Holmes and Starling, who were now standing in front of the fire.

'What has become of the valet?' Holmes demanded to know.

A distorted laugh emerged from behind the mask and Gruner waved us towards the chairs with his gun before answering.

'Unfortunately, the poor fellow will not be able to join us, Herr Holmes. Perhaps you will soon share in his unfortunate fate?' The familiar voice, although distorted by the damage caused by the oil of vitriol, had lost none of its maliciousness and we all knew the true meaning behind Gruner's ironic response.

'I remember once warning you that to cross my path was not a lucky thing to do,[16] and I am afraid that your friend has learned that to his great cost. I assume that it is not necessary for me to hide my identity from you any longer?'

Holmes and I shook our heads emphatically and the 'Austrian murderer' slowly untied and removed his mask.

You can be certain that, during my tour of duty in Afghanistan as an army surgeon, I had been a reluctant witness to many a horrific wound and injury. However, none of these could have prepared me for the pitiable facial deformities that the removal of Gruner's mask now revealed. Against our better judgement and natures, each one of us, save Holmes of course, had released an involuntary gasp of

---

[16] From 'The Four-Handed Game' by P.D.G. and 'The Adventure of the Final Problem' by Sir A.C.D.

revulsion at the sight of Gruner's damage, and he laughed ironically at our inability to suppress them.

The oil of vitriol had stripped away almost half of the Baron's facial skin, and his left eye was barely supported by the remains of its socket. His lips were twisted into a purple contortion and his hair had been reduced to a few dead stalks. Every one of his facial movements accentuated the severity of his wounds and when he had laughed, the damaged flesh seemed to be stretched to its limits.

'You see, Mr Holmes, the sorry state to which you have reduced me? Oh, you could argue of course that I received my retribution from another source, and that she had been fully justified in her actions. Nevertheless, it had been your constant interference that had led to that scenario in the first place and your persecution of me continues still it seems.' Miss Vukovic's attempts at breaking free interrupted Gruner's tirade and he tightened his grip on her throat and pulled back the hammer of his gun.

'So help me, Mr Holmes, I shall blow this witch's head off if you do not produce my papers immediately!'

'In heaven's name, Holmes, hand him over the papers. A woman's life is at stake!' I exclaimed, forgetting for a moment that they were safely locked away back in London.

Still my friend remained unrelenting and Gruner moved towards us menacingly, while his grip upon Miss Vukovic remained tight and threatening.

'Do not think for one minute that I shall hesitate in turning my gun upon the rest of you once I am done with her?' He jerked her head back violently by her hair, as if to emphasise a violent intent that was already quite obvious.

'You see, Mr Holmes, I really do have nothing left to lose. You have taken my face, my plans for a better future, and my daughter. Now please, place any weapons that you might possess on the floor and slide them away.' Regretfully, I kicked my revolver across the floor to the far side of the room and Gruner visibly relaxed for a moment.

'That was very sensible of you, Dr Watson, but I hope your colleague will display the same good sense by returning to me my property!' Gruner raised his distorted voice to a new manic level and his hideous facial contortions were impossible even to look upon.

At that moment, a door that led to the opposite wing, at the far end of the room, very slowly began to open and a familiar shape filled the frame. He bent down to pick up my revolver and raised it in the direction of our assailant.

'I think not, Herr Gruner. Perhaps you should drop *your* weapon instead?' In disbelief, we all turned towards the booming voice of Mycroft Holmes!

'No, it is impossible!' Gruner screamed as he pushed Miss Vukovic violently away from him. The odious man turned his gun towards my friend as he sought his final and desperate attempt at vengeance upon his tormentor.

The sound of a solitary shot rang out, and simultaneously a bloody hole appeared in the back of Gruner's disfigured head. His gun fell to the floor and while emitting a final howl of frustration, the 'Austrian murderer' breathed his last upon the floor of Mycroft Holmes's lodge!

'Brother Mycroft, I am glad to note that you still possess a most steady hand.' Holmes smiled and at once I became consumed by the notion that my friend had not been as surprised as the rest of us at the welcome sight of his brother.

My head reverberated with a myriad of questions, but obviously these would have to await the conclusion of all of the formalities. At once, my friend instigated a search for the driver that Gruner had so surreptitiously replaced. Though bound and gagged, mercifully he was found alive and well, and concealed beneath some large bales of hay within the barn. Once he had been warmed and revived by a large glass of cognac, Mycroft despatched him to bring the authorities from nearby Drumnadrochit. Naturally, the lawyer had decided to return with him, for the miraculous 'resurrection' of Mycroft Holmes had rendered his intended function at the lodge redundant.

Although the blizzard had now abated, the treacherous conditions had rendered the journey a long and hazardous one, and so we moved Gruner's body to the far side of the room while we awaited the driver's return. The body of the valet had not been so easy to find. Of course, Miss Vukovic had been with him at the beginning of their search for the driver, and Gruner had come upon her from an area behind the barn. However, the valet had met his fate a few feet beyond the barn, where the wind had picked up the snow and piled it into a huge drift.

The three of us, together with a large shovel, eventually discovered the poor fellow with a gunshot wound to his forehead, and we struggled with him back into the lodge to await the wagon. This proved to be some time in coming, and we sat there in a stunned and pensive silence until its arrival. Such had been the aura of Mycroft's influence and reputation that the authorities barely batted an eyelid at the notion of removing two dead bodies from his lodge, although he did assure them that he would subsequently clarify the matter upon his next visit to town. They merely bowed in quiet deference, removed the bodies, and then went about their business.

After closing the door behind them, Mycroft rubbed his hands together in a display of insensible satisfaction and brought out his brandy decanter and four glasses. This scenario was reminiscent of that night within the royal hunting lodge in Bavaria, and I could not help but consider how long ago those events seemed to have been.

With our drinks now poured and our cigars alight, I leant forward and eyed the two Holmes brothers with a most quizzical and recriminatory eye.

'It would seem that the unique ability of successfully simulating one's own death is a skill that runs throughout your family,' I said accusingly, alluding, of course, to the events subsequent to my friend's fateful confrontation with the late Professor Moriarty at the Reichenbach Falls.[17]

---

[17]   From 'The Adventure of the Final Problem' by Sir A.C.D.

It had been gratifying for me to observe how both of the Holmes brothers shuffled uncomfortably in their chairs before my friend picked up the baton of having to placate me. Miss Vukovic could barely conceal her amusement at their discomfort.

'Obviously,' began Holmes, 'my brother will have his own explanation for his act of subterfuge, but I can assure you, Watson, that I had absolutely no prior knowledge of his intentions until I had observed the bearers at the graveside. Despite the employment of an appropriately oversized coffin, I could see at once that the depth, to which the bearer's steel-toed boots sank in the soft lying snow, did not, by any stretch of the imagination, correspond to the weight of my brother. My reaction to that letter, from Starling, Williamson and Starling, was completely genuine and I had been as ignorant as you as to my brother's devious machinations. Therefore, I shall leave to him the task of further enlightening you, although I am certain that Miss Vukovic would be just as capable as he.' Holmes smiled at Ara as he handed the honour over to his brother with a broad sweep of his arm.

While Mycroft tried to conceal his bluster behind a thick flume of cigar smoke, I interjected with a question of my own.

'Although I am delighted and relieved to see that Mycroft clearly was not in his own coffin, it does beggar the question of who actually was inside it. Even I could see that the coffin had not been an empty one.'

'Excellent, Dr Watson, for that indeed had been my intention. I had been certain that all those present would have been similarly deceived, apart from my brother, of course, and his discovery of my little ploy did nothing to detract from its success.'

'I fail to see how this afternoon's performance might be viewed as any kind of a success,' I insisted.

'Ah, but you see it was an absolute triumph, and the events that led to the formulation of my deception rendered it to be all the more so. Shortly after we had settled in at my little abode, I received news from my people that the Gruners trail had at last been picked up again. Furthermore, they had been observed here in the Highlands of Scotland, obviously with the intention of reclaiming their vital property.

'We at once recognised the threat that this news had placed us under, and we set about the task of securing the property and its perimeters without a moment's delay. Miss Vukovic has been invaluable to me throughout, and I am certain that were it not for her bravery and vigilance, I should not be here today.

'My people finally lost sight of the Gruners once they had arrived at Drumnadrochit, and we knew that their assault would, in all likelihood, be an imminent one. During the course of that day we boarded up the unused west wing of the building, thereby reducing our area of defence. The stable hand together with my unfortunate valet, John Vardy, kept watch outside until the early dusk finally fell, and then we doused the entire building in total darkness.

'Despite all of our precautions, the Gruners had managed to elude our various traps and alarms, and our ears were now straining for any indication of their advance. The intense silence heightened our senses, and all of our weapons were primed and at the ready. The shutters on each of the windows had been closed and secured, save one.

'Sure enough, almost on the stroke of midnight, it was towards this unprotected opening that the Gruners had decided to make their approach. For them the weather had proven to be a double-edged sword. The dense and immobile cloud cover had eliminated the risk of their being illuminated by the moon, but the layer of frost that sat upon the settled snow meant that a silent footstep would be an impossibility.

'We had previously decided that the best method for successfully apprehending this felonious family would be to allow them to gain access to the lodge and then to surprise them with a sudden injection of light, and, of course, our weapons. The complete darkness outside would have created too many imponderables and so we decided to wait indoors.

The sound of boots upon snow soon became increasingly audible and my hand moved towards the oil lamp on the table closest to the window.

'There had been a brief pause while they decided on the best means of gaining access and then, once the decision had been made, the long slim blade of a knife came into view as it began to search for the catch upon the sash. This process took an agonising age to execute, and my hand had been positively aching by the time that they finally achieved success.

'The knife had been silently withdrawn before the lower half of the window slowly began to rise. Still we kept our nerve and eventually our patience was rewarded by the sight of a boot and leg easing its way through the ever-increasing gap. The sudden rush of cold night air took our breaths away, especially as the fire had long since been extinguished, but we held fast.

'To our great surprise, the first person to have crept through the window had not been the one that we had been expecting to see. Baron Gruner's devious maliciousness has never been in doubt, but I was appalled to note that he had now added cowardice to his long list of flaws. For there, standing before us, with that knife in elegant hand, stood the tall, slender form of his daughter, Diana.

'She moved through the window and across the floor with the dexterity and grace of a gazelle, and she had even started the search for those papers before her father finally ventured to follow her path. Disastrously, it was at that precise moment that the cold blast of air caused John Vardy to emit an ill-suppressed sneeze, which had alerted the Gruners at once!

'In an attempt at reclaiming the situation, I turned the lamp on immediately and switched round the light into the astonished face of Gruner's daughter. Her treacherous father had turned on his heels at once and made for his horse, without even a second glance towards his beleaguered daughter. To her credit, Miss Gruner displayed a bravery and loyalty, although misguided at best, that allowed her father the time to beat his hasty retreat.

'With all thoughts of reclaiming the papers now banished, Diana decided to vent her anger upon the person closest to her, and lunged towards me while brandishing her long and deadly blade and emitting the scream of a banshee!

'Fortunately for me, Miss Vukovic's nerve held firm and with a single shot she brought down the deluded child when her blade was barely a hair's breadth away from my skin!' Mycroft paused his narrative for a moment, as he needed to draw breath after passing on these dramatic recollections.

'Dr Watson, I am certain that by now you do not need me to tell you who had occupied my coffin in my stead?' he asked mischievously.

'No indeed, it was undoubtedly that tragic and misguided heroine, Diana Gruner,' I confirmed. 'However, you have still not explained why you considered any subsequent masquerade to have been necessary in the first place,' I pointed out.

'Although not necessary, Dr Watson, I did consider that the opportunity that this incident had provided me with was indeed a most desirable and fortuitous one. It immediately occurred to me that I should be able to work with far more freedom and security, if as many interested parties as possible were to think that I was dead. Consequently, I instructed Starling, Williamson and Starling to send notice to all members of the Diogenes Club, together with those who had previously worked with me in Whitehall that had not fully earned my confidence. I trust,' Mycroft said with a mischievous smile, 'that you were both surprised at the size of the gathering for the funeral of a crotchety old recluse, were you not?'

'I must confess that it was somewhat larger than even I could have foreseen, although I am certain that you would have undoubtedly achieved the effect that you had desired. Perhaps those whom you previously held under suspicion will now behave with a little less discretion?' Holmes suggested.

'One would certainly hope so, Sherlock, although ours still remains an enormous and unenviable task.'

'How do you intend to utilise this newly won freedom of yours?' Holmes asked.

'By acquiring and then passing on to you and Dr Watson as much useful information as I can glean. Of course, we already have the advantage of being in possession of Gruner's papers and, of course, his death will have set back the plans of the Austrian cell of the Brotherhood considerably. However, that cell is only one of the many ugly heads that form this particular Hydra, and our task must be to slice each one from its neck every time that a new aberration might reveal itself,' Mycroft concluded with determination.

'Watson,' said Holmes, 'it is absolutely vital that we maintain our humble practice, although all the while we must maintain a vigilant eye on any new mobilisations of the Brotherhood. After all, we are only too well aware of their future intentions and the size of the stakes that we are playing for. Are you up for the challenge old friend?'

'Well, of course I am!' I exclaimed.

'Capital, capital! Now gentlemen, and lady, of course,' said Mycroft, 'I propose one last glass of this most excellent cognac before we retire for the night. I suggest an early departure, Sherlock, for any delay in your return to London will surely give rise to some undesirable and unnecessary suspicions.'

We all nodded our consent and consumed our drinks with gusto. Throughout this exchange I noticed, once again, how my friend had maintained an intense and suspicious examination of Miss Vukovic. Admittedly she had remained in an impassive silence, but I thought it to be quite understandable under those circumstances. Perhaps, once again, she felt unsure of her intended role in all of this? In any event, she joined the procession upstairs and before long all of the lights had been doused and the doors closed.

I slept fitfully that night and my head was constantly reverberating with each one of Mycroft's auspicious words. Time and again I gave up the comfort of my bed and sat by the window with a cigarette and a carafe of water. I glanced at my watch on countless occasions and thus I had been fully awake and alert when, at the stroke of four, the sounds of a violent commotion emanated from the room next to my own.

I tightened the cord to my dressing gown and grabbed my gun, for the adjacent room belonged to my friend, Sherlock Holmes. I did not hesitate in barging the door open with my shoulder, but upon doing so I had been left in a state of utter bewilderment by the unnerving and bizarre sight with which I had been confronted.

There, sprawled upon the hearth rug, lay Miss Vukovic, with my friend straddled across her while pinning her shoulders down with his knees! All the while they were struggling for the possession of a murderous-looking knife which the young assassin clung to with a manic tenacity.

Her intent was clear, and yet it was a moment or two before my senses could take in this surreal sight and act upon it. Finally, when Holmes turned towards me with an impatient glare, I strode forward and brandished my revolver in front of the hysterical woman's face. She let out a high-pitched shriek before loosening her hold upon the knife with a frustrated resignation.

I picked up the weapon from the floor and stood back while Holmes gradually released her from his vice-like grip. I gestured towards a chair with my gun and Miss Vukovic grudgingly took the seat while emitting a tirade of angry expletives, thankfully in her own tongue.

'Stop this at once and explain to me the meaning behind all of this madness!' I exclaimed, while inadvertently waving my gun in her face once more.

'Is it not obvious to you, Watson?' said Holmes. 'This young harpy has tried her best to kill your old friend in his bed, and came damn well close to succeeding, I should add.' Holmes swept his hair back from his forehead and stood over her with a surprising smile of admiration.

'You seem surprisingly calm, Holmes,' I ventured.

'He seemed to be expecting my attack, Dr Watson,' said Ara. 'I had no great difficulty in picking this simple lock, but as I crept closer to his bed, I realised that the shape beneath the sheets was nothing more than just a pile of his clothing. By then, of course, it was too late, and despite my best efforts he soon overcame me and got me to the floor.' Her frustration and anger had given way to a calm resignation, and she stared up at my friend with benign esteem.

'But why would you have attempted such a thing?'

Miss Vukovic refused to answer me, and I turned to Holmes in desperation.

'I am more interested to find out how he came to know of my plans,' Miss Vukovic enquired.

'Young lady, that is easier to explain than you might think, and I can also resolve your confusion, Watson, with the same rationalization. The answer, as ever, lies is the power of observation, and once again, my friend, you have failed to exercise yours.

'You see, I never truly believed that potted history of her life which she so eloquently expounded while we were on the train together, simply because her Germanic accent and mannerisms were just too good. Obviously, she is a woman of honour and loyalty, qualities which my brother could not have failed to have recognised, but perhaps at times these are a little bit misguided?

'In any event, I was certain by now that she suspected me of harbouring my reservations, and no doubt hoped that they would have been allayed by the manner in which she defended my brother. As a matter of fact, they were actually heightened when I observed the relish with which she had greeted the demise of Baron Gruner. Therefore, once I had seen how discreetly she had refrained from the delights of the cognac decanter, I felt certain that she was planning her attack for tonight.' Holmes lit a cigarette with a self-satisfied smile that implied that he had satisfactorily explained every detail.

'My dear Holmes,' I ejaculated, 'you have still not explained why she should have attempted such a dastardly deed.'

'Oh, but is it not now obvious? Watson, when have you ever seen such intense green eyes matched with a fiery head of red hair? They belonged to a man who had gone to such great lengths to ensnare the notorious Baron and who was also a mortal enemy of the Brotherhood. Think man!' Holmes implored while Miss Vukovic nodded her appreciation of my friend's reasoning.

My head was humming with confusion, for the only name that sprang to my mind was that of Theodore Daxer, he of such ill repute.

'In all honesty, Watson, I cannot truly blame Miss Vukovic for her attempted act of vengeance; after all, I did cause the death of her father . . .'

CHAPTER SIXTEEN

221B BAKER STREET

'It is still beyond my comprehension, Sherlock, that you have entrusted Mycroft into the tender care of one who had previously come so close to a murderous act of treachery against his brother,' I protested towards the conclusion of our first breakfast, once back at Baker Street.

'You think that I have behaved in a frivolous manner with regard to my brother's welfare?' Holmes asked, before draining the last remnants from his coffee cup.

'Most certainly I do! Miss Vukovic has certainly proved herself to be unworthy of trust, and she is obviously a woman of a most violent disposition. Undoubtedly she has great courage, and she is certainly highly skilled in her dark arts, but for you to assume that Mycroft is secure in her company is to treat his safety in a most cavalier fashion,' I insisted.

Holmes eyed me quizzically over the rim of his cup, before slowly lowering it down to its saucer.

'My dear fellow, I am afraid that when it comes to an appraisal of my character, you have sadly erred. Although Mycroft and I have never been exactly close, you should also know that I have always held him in the highest regard and, therefore, would never knowingly place his life in jeopardy. What you view as an act of treachery, I see as an act of loyalty to the memory of her late father. That particular character trait ensures that the gratitude she feels towards my brother will always guarantee her steadfast devotion to his cause. Mycroft's faith in her saved Miss Vukovic from a life on the streets, and she believes that she owes him much.'

'Even her life?'

'Yes, even her life,' Holmes confirmed, before turning his attention towards the fire and his pipe.

'Considering your well-documented mistrust of the fairer sex, you seem to be bestowing upon Miss Vukovic a most uncharacteristic aura of admiration and esteem,' I continued, although now in a more mischievous tone, which was not lost upon my friend.

He threw down the fire tongs, with which he had just lit his pipe, with an obvious display of pique and growled out his reply through clenched teeth.

'Watson, as I have told you on countless occasions, I have never shared your admiration of the allures of the countless number of young ladies who have passed through our doors over the years. However, I would be a poor logician indeed were I not to acknowledge the existence of that rarity, a woman of accomplishment and resolute character.

'I can assure you, Doctor, that despite your intimation to the contrary, I only view Miss Vukovic from a practical and professional viewpoint and therefore, with an unclouded judgement, I can assess the value that she might be to us throughout the daunting challenges that still lie ahead.'

'Well, of course you must have it your own way, but I am sure that even your icy blood must have been at least momentarily stirred by her singularly striking appearance.'

Holmes ignored my final attempt at coaxing an admission from him and he immediately returned my fire with a barbed attack of his own.

'I assume that it shall not be too long before your thoughts and attentions turn towards West Hampstead and a certain young actress who resides there?'

'It is just possible, I suppose, but for now all of my considerations revolve around our receiving fresh news from Drumnadrochit,' I replied with an air of false nonchalance.

In truth, I had thought of little else since our return to London, and the only misgivings that had held me back this long had been the actual motives behind any potential visit to Sophie Sinclair. Were I to do so, then I needed to be certain of my true intentions, and perhaps I had also been a little wary of her reaction, or lack of reciprocation, were I to betray my true feelings.

'That is indeed most admirable, friend Watson, most admirable.' Holmes smiled and we sank back into a reflective silence in front of the fire.

You will no doubt recall how Holmes had expressed the importance of our continuing with his practice, despite having to maintain our vigilance against the potential threat still posed by the Brotherhood. My published chronicles of his cases had inevitably brought him into the public domain and he feared that any deviation from our customary behaviour might generate some unwelcome attention from our enemies.

As reasonable as this suggestion might have seemed at first, its execution proved to be somewhat harder to achieve. The day of epiphany came and went, and Holmes and I spent much of the month of January in sheltering by our fire from the intense cold, while waiting impatiently for our next case or some news from Mycroft.

Neither had been immediately forthcoming and my records show that throughout that long and dismal month, the only matter of interest to be brought to our door had been the remarkable and singular case of 'The Treasure of the Poison King', an adventure that I shall shortly include in my chronicles.

This prolonged period of inactivity inevitably produced in my friend one of his brown moods and frequent displays of melancholic irritation that were both unwarranted and intolerable. Consequently, on a particularly cold and frosty afternoon, and when the toxicity in our rooms had plunged to new depths, I decided to ignore my chariness and made for West Hampstead with a steely resolve.

By the time that I had alighted from my train, with chapped lips and chattering teeth, my new-found inner strength had all but dissolved. I found myself pacing back and forth along the platform, and on each turn I realised that I was no closer to a resolution. In fact, I had been on the point of boarding the very next train back to Baker Street, when a jolly and familiar voice caused me to withdraw.

At once I had recognised the tall and upright figure of young Simon Sinclair, brother of the subject of my dilemma, and he appeared to have been as confused as he had been glad to see me there. His smile and cheery demeanour went some way towards dispelling the worst of my fears, and he ran forward to take my hand.

'Dr Watson, I cannot in all truth imagine that you would be planning to depart from West Hampstead without having first called upon my sister? It must have been on a most urgent mission indeed for you to have committed such an oversight,' Sinclair suggested, once we had exchanged the customary pleasantries.

His tone had suggested that he had managed to divine the cause of my indecision, and even before the young man had finished speaking, I began to realise just how ridiculous my behaviour must have seemed and how absurd had been my caution.

'My sister and I have spent a most delightful afternoon together, and I do believe that I might have spared you a scone or two, if you are quick!' he suggested amiably.

Then he lowered his voice, moved closer towards me, and adopted a more sincere tone.

'My sister speaks of you often, Dr Watson.' Simon Sinclair doffed his hat and pointed towards his sister's apartment before boarding the train.

With his words still echoing in my ears, I strode off quickly and determinedly in the direction that he had just indicated and I had arrived at Miss Sinclair's doorstep breathless and flushed. My condition had been due to the harsh conditions, rather than my state of nerves, and I awaited the opening door with a renewed confidence and great anticipation.

A moment later I realised that my earlier trepidation had been totally unwarranted. Sophie Sinclair greeted me with a warm smile, such as I had not experienced in many a long and lonely year. She took my hand with a soft assurance as she led me through the door, and before too long I began to feel strangely at home.

No doubt you will excuse my outmoded sense of chivalry at this juncture, for I shall not describe within these pages that which transpired between myself and a young lady, alone within her rooms. Suffice it to say that by the time I had departed I had been left in little doubt that Miss Sinclair had reciprocated my feelings and that our future together was assured.

I was equally resolved, however, that our coming together would have to be delayed, until such time as the threat posed by the Brotherhood had been removed, or at the least, reduced. It was not until the following morning, when back at Baker Street, that I was to realise just what a labour this undertaking of ours was to be.

Holmes had retired by the time that I had finally made my return; therefore, it was not until breakfast the following morning that I was to receive his inevitable rebuke.

'You know, Watson, I really cannot, in all honesty, congratulate you,' he stated simply and dispassionately.

I did not ask him to detail the reasoning behind his statement, for on this occasion no miraculous deductive powers would have been necessary in ascertaining my mood and frame of mind, much less the cause of such a transformation.

I let my cutlery fall angrily down upon my empty plate and glared up at my friend, who sat there with a characteristic, enigmatic air.

'Well, I really did not expect anything better from you!' I exclaimed. 'You have greeted the prospect of my future happiness with the same expression of selfishness that you subjected me to when my dear Mary first came into my life.'

To my great surprise, Holmes seemed to be visibly shocked and disappointed by my outburst.

'You misunderstand me, Watson, although perhaps not without good reason.' I did not detect any of that sardonic lilt to his voice that I might otherwise have anticipated, and I decided to hear him out without resorting to any premature display of annoyance.

'As you know, only too well,' said he, 'I have not been and never shall be a proponent or an advocate of the institution of marriage. Nevertheless, the many years that I have spent in studying the nature and behaviour of the human animal have proven to me its value to the progression and evolution of the species. Equally so, I am now willing to admit to and acknowledge its potential meretricious effects upon the individual . . .'

At this point I could no longer contain my laughter. To hear Sherlock Holmes extol the virtues of such an emotional and romantic tradition in terms so scientific and pragmatic was too much for me to bear, and I drowned him out most uproariously! My friend was noticeably put out.

'Well, I certainly had not expected my long-considered admission to have been greeted with such derision and amusement. Nevertheless, I will conclude by informing you that my lack of congratulations was born more of its timing rather than the actuality of your proposed union with Miss Sinclair.'

By way of an explanation, Holmes tossed over to me a buff foolscap envelope that had been scrawled upon by his brother Mycroft. I removed the letter with a reluctant anticipation.

No one could ever have accused Mycroft Holmes of brevity or succinctness, and, consequently, I shall not try my reader's patience by attempting to reproduce the letter here. Nonetheless, my desire to précis his words should not detract from their weight and consequence. In brief, he wished to inform us that both he and Miss Vukovic remained well and that there had been no further indication of the Brotherhood in the region around Inverness.

Obviously, our enemies had been dealt a smart blow by the loss of their papers and the subsequent demise of Baron Gruner. Indeed, Mycroft surmised, the Austrian cell of the Brotherhood would take some considerable time in recovering fully. However, we should not be lulled into a false sense of security.

The banking house that had both financed them and consequently directed them, was growing in strength and influence at an alarming rate, and their plans, of which we had seen only the briefest glimpse, had been set back only myopically. Indeed, Mycroft's continued research into both Bohemian Grove and its auspicious members had gone some way to confirming the validity of each one of our writer friend's 'fictitious' predications.

I let out a low whistle as I considered each word of Mycroft's dire appraisal, a display that had not gone unnoticed by my friend.

'My brother does not exactly paint an optimistic vision, eh Watson? However, please read on, for his projections do not improve.' My friend had tried to bury his concerns beneath an air of bravado, but with only a minimal success. He offered me one of his cigarettes and we both breathed in the smoke with a feverish enthusiasm.

At certain junctures, Mycroft's verbosity tended to cloud over the significance of his concerns, but in essence he was now in no doubt that the first two of those predicted worldwide cataclysms were now unavoidable and unstoppable, despite our being so forewarned. Nevertheless, he was equally convinced that we were more than capable of diluting the desired long-term effects of these conflicts; as they were due to occur in the not too distant future and we already knew of their ultimate goal.

There was equally no doubt that the prophetic book, to which we had all attached such great significance, could indeed prove to be a most suitable warning for those to come, should it be widely read. Therefore, Mycroft implored me to delay the publication of my own accounts until such time as he deemed appropriate. This request had been made as much out of regard for our safety as it had been for the security of his long-term plans.

> *In the meantime, continue with your everyday routines while remaining ever vigilant and aware. Above all, stay safe and well.*
>
> *Your brother,*
> *Mycroft Holmes.*

Holmes and I had sat in silence by the fire for an indeterminable length of time and we had only been alerted to the lateness of the hour by the sound of the dying embers crumbling into the cooling grate. Throughout that time, I had thought of nothing other than the form in which any future account of mine might take.

Only now had I been able to appreciate the full significance of our investigations in Rome, Egypt, and Bavaria. The myriad of cases, with which we had been bombarded upon our return to London, had all led us to this most momentous of junctures, and I also realised that perhaps that awful and considerable loss of life, from that of Shenouda to the villainous Roger Ashley, et al., had not entirely been in vain.

At this point I should assure my more observant readers that I have transposed the date of my account of the Baron Gruner affair to a time that would not jeopardise the anonymity of the true 'Illustrious Client'. Therefore, in that same spirit of discretion, I have withheld the name of our prophetic author, together with the identity of the banking house that had been responsible for many of the insidious activities that we were attempting to thwart. Obviously, I will refrain from releasing these later accounts until such time as Mycroft deems it to be appropriate and beneficial.

Mercifully, it had been on the following morning that the mystery of 'The Treasure of the Poison King' had been brought to our door. Although this matter had proven to be a case of both considerable interest and one that had also presented to Holmes its own set of peculiar and appealing challenges, it had also served as a most welcome diversion from the long and anxious wait that we had hitherto been enduring.

Upon its satisfactory conclusion, Holmes suggested that we celebrate our success with a sumptuous meal and a bottle of wine at Simpson's, a proposal with which I most heartily concurred. A short while later we were tucking into that renowned eatery's famous game pie, accompanied by a very fine bottle of Calvet.

On our return to Baker Street, we sank back into our chairs and indulged in that feeling of satisfaction and fulfilment which comes from a full stomach and a slight redness of cheek. Holmes suddenly turned towards me, and he bore the appearance of one who had just experienced an epiphany.

'I must say, Watson, that although you may not possess the mental dexterity of a logician, and are somewhat lacking in the finer arts of observation and deduction, I can think of no other man alive with whom I would rather share my adventures, nor into whose hands I would entrust my life with such impunity.'

I searched his facial expression for a trace of insincerity, but there was none. However, this momentary display of human empathy had disappeared within the blink of an eye and as he faced forward once more, he did so with a steely intensity and resolve, as if the immediate future was already mapped out clearly in his mind.

Nevertheless, I would forever treasure that moment. My good friend, Sherlock Holmes, had finally voiced his appreciation of my contributions and I felt proud of the fact that I had been allowed to associate with the foremost champion of justice of this, or any other, age.

Therefore, and for the first time in quite a while, I felt optimistic for the future.

THE END

ALSO BY PAUL D. GILBERT

THE ODYSSEY OF
SHERLOCK HOLMES SERIES

BOOK 1: *Sherlock Holmes and the Unholy Trinity*
BOOK 2: *Sherlock Holmes: The Four-Handed Game*
BOOK 3: *The Illumination of Sherlock Holmes*

THE LOST FILES OF
SHERLOCK HOLMES SERIES

BOOK 1: *The Lost Files of Sherlock Holmes*
BOOK 2: *The Chronicles of Sherlock Holmes*
BOOK 3: *The Annals of Sherlock Holmes*

STANDALONE NOVELS
Sherlock Holmes and the Giant Rat of Sumatra

Don't miss the latest Paul D. Gilbert release,
join our mailing list:

www.joffebooks.com

READ MORE BOOKS

Please join our mailing list for free Kindle books and new releases, including crime thrillers, mysteries, romance and more!

www.joffebooks.com

Thank you for reading this book. If you enjoyed it please leave feedback on Amazon, and if there is anything we missed or you have a question about then please get in touch.

Follow us on facebook www.facebook.com/joffebooks

We're very grateful to eagle-eyed readers who take the time to contact us. Please send any errors you find to corrections@joffebooks.com

47866244R00106

Printed in Poland
by Amazon Fulfillment
Poland Sp. z o.o., Wrocław